# Vision of the Field: A Baseball Fantasy

## By

## Joe Kaminski, Jr.

ISBN: 978-0-6151-3538-0

VISION OF THE FIELD: A BASEBALL FANTASY

This Book is dedicated to all my friends and family who helped and supported me during my long recovery from my heart-lung transplant

CHAPTER ONE: THE INTRO

I still can't believe it. If I only had heard of it, I would have said, hell, it didn't happen. But there it was. After all, I wrote the story. He had a dream, to play baseball and he did.

Flying into Chicago that day, I was filled with both anticipation and a lot of questions. I was also skeptical. I wondered what exactly was the reason I was going to cover a no-talent baseball player who had never played a big league game in his life.

My name is Rob Sweeney, I write for a paper in Mesa Arizona. I've been a sports writer for twenty years. Until five years ago, I wrote for a Chicago newspaper. But, a scandal ensued and I finally ended up here, with the heat, Gila monsters, and a bad professional football team. It's not a bad job, but, sometimes I feel more like a stringer on a large city paper, rather than a well- known sports writer, like I was when I was in Chicago.

Now, I always loved of journalism and writing. I remember how much I liked journalism class in high school. At the Catholic school where I attended, the nun who taught the class would insist on the proper way to get the facts of a story out. One of her favorite lines was "where's the dope," meaning where's the facts,

I would mutter to myself, "check the equipment room," That's where more than athletic equipment was stored. The jocks would use the place to smoke and drink. I should know since I was the equipment manager for the school.

Joyce, the gal who sat behind me in class, would poke me and whisper "Hey! Shut up! Do you want Sister to hear you?" I would just snicker. But what can I say. It was the seventies!

I lived in Hegwhisch and as a child and had a regular childhood, doing the usual things that a boy does like getting into mischief and trying not to get blamed. I was not a great student in school, but I still learned a lot. I went to a Catholic grade school, where the nuns (yep, we still had them when I was going!) would have pulled their hair out, if they didn't have the veils. The only thing I loved, besides sports, was writing and drawing weather maps.

Everyone thought I would become a weatherman, but sports won out and combined with my writing became the perfect combination for a successful career.

I also went to a Catholic high school that was across the border in Hammond, Indiana. Many times I would take the bus from the school into North Hammond, then walk the bumpy, curvy road back to Hegwhisch and my favorite record shop to buy some cheap albums to listen on those days when there was nothing to do.

I often called the road 'the road between nothingness and nowhere.' It seemed to go on forever and only became shorter once I learned how to drive. Then it became bumpier and curvier.

In high school I hung around three groups of people. Each group was different in their own way. I hung with a few of the jocks, partly because I was the equipment manager and I knew their secrets. A lot of them could have been suspended if I told the coaches and teachers what they did when the coaches weren't looking. Come to think of it the coaches would have been fired if anything had come out. So I was assured of a nice welcome any time I came around.

The second group was just regular students. All of them were good people. They weren't all the brains of the school, although some of them were pretty smart. But they gave me a lot of laughs and it was pretty much the group I hung out because they were regular kids.

I also had a group of intellectual friends, who enjoyed writing, science and science fiction, philosophy and a little journalism. I remember when some of them started an Underground Paper at the school (remember this was the early seventies, Viet Nam War and all). It caused a real riot in the school. Teachers trying to find out who was publishing the paper: who was distributing it (I was)? Who was responsible (we all were)?

One friend of mine got quite a bit of fame and notoriety for his writing. Some how, the English teachers fell in love with him. To this day, I don't really understand why. He once wrote a short story called 'The Twelve Gateways and 7/8.' I think he read a little too much of Poe and watched too much of Kubrick's '2001.' The teachers, however, loved it.

That short story and a play where he had God sitting on his throne surrounded by all the angels and drinking grape juice, made him a celebrity on campus.

What all of them didn't know that while all of this was going on, I was watching a kid going slowly nuts. I figured he went off the deep end the day he legally changed his name from Paul Bosky to Crimean Solcrum.

He spent most of his time in his room at home writing and even got a College Professor interested in his work. They would sit around hours discussing his progress and how he could become a great writer along the likes of Steinbeck, Hemmingway Fitzgerald. Nobody ever cared to notice that perhaps he was losing his mind.

Maybe all these teachers and professors meant well, but I thought they should have seen the end before it came. They didn't and the end result was a wasted talent and a wasted life,

One day I came to see Crimean, err, Paul. I went to visit him up in his room at his parent's house. There he was working on another great masterpiece. He was so into what he was doing that he did not notice that I had came into the room. He just continued writing and talking to himself. "You got it, Crimean." He would say as he wrote one part or another.

He said he was surprised when he at last looked up and saw me there. Was he faking it, I don't know. But I do know that while I am writing this I am not asking myself anything out loud or answering either.

The last time I saw Paul (face it I can't call him Crimean), was my sophomore year in College. I had just come home from my part time job when my Mom said "Paul is in the basement, just sitting there reading, He says he has a proposal for you." She looked a little scared.

I went down and said hi and asked him what was so important, He asked me to consider joining him in establishing a writer's commune. He wanted me to quit school, get all my cash together and become a resident writer as part of a communal experiment. I drew up all 5'9"of me and told him "Join a commune? I'm having too much fun already, doing what I'm doing,"

Paul wasn't happy with my response, but he didn't get angry. He told me that he was disappointed in me, but I had to do what I had to do. To show me that he wasn't mad he gave me all his prized Beatles and Credence Clearwater Revival albums. I protested, but he said that where he was going he didn't need then, how true he spoke.

I never talked with Paul again. I would see him tooling around on his bicycle and before I really knew what had happened, he sort of disappeared. A few years later, I saw his parents when I came home for a visit. I asked him how Paul was and they just shook their heads. Seems that the voices in Paul's head became a little too much for him. His parents, fearing the worst for him, had him committed. Occasionally he would be released, but invariably he would have to go back. It was a sad end to a sad life.

I played sports in high school, I wasn't very good, and so, I rode the bench a lot. After figuring out that I was never going to amount to any thing as an athlete, I decided that I should just be an equipment manager for the school. It kept me involved with the guys on the teams and I used my contacts to write sports stories for the newspaper.

You would think I would go to a nice university when I got out of high school, but no, not me. I went to a local Catholic college yet, where they had atmosphere. They used storefronts for their classrooms and an old water plant for their theater. It was the best investment I could have made. I soaked up the atmosphere and learned a lot writing and photography while working in the newspaper and the yearbook.

Any way, back to the story. Max Bennet, the sports editor for the Mesa paper called me to his office, from across the room. Now Max was bald, a little dumpy and pretty much your Lou Grant type, without the charm. He was known to enjoy a good stiff whiskey from a bottle that he kept in his desk. I suppose that's how the Lou Grant image came to be. If you could get through his gruffness, he was ok. I suppose being an editor on a small city paper for a number of years would make one a bit grouchy at times. He had once been a hotshot reporter during the Korean War. He had even won a number of awards for his writing.

But he got tired of writing about wars and death. So when he had the chance, he got out of writing those types of stories and became a sports writer, where the stories weren't as exciting, but there was a loss less death and destruction.

Like his earlier writing, he excelled in sports writing, winning a number of awards and getting a chance to be a regular on a TV sports program called "The Sports Reporters," based out of Los Angeles.

When he got tired of all of that Max Bennet took the job as a sports editor for the Mesa Gazette. It may have not seemed to be as exciting as being a big time sports reporter, but, underneath it all, Max got a thrill seeing young reporters come into their own and make a name for themselves. Just don't let him know that you know that. He would rather be known as a grouchy old cuss.

I get in his office and he says to me "Got an assignment for you. I want you to go to Chicago and cover a baseball player for the Chicago Cubs."

"Huh?" I say, "Why would you want me to do that? What's the big deal?"

Max said, "well, it seems this guy who they're going to bring up, or something, was a heart transplant recipient an I guess the big shots in the Tribune organization are going to let him take part in one game next week, The big shot is a friend of our publisher and they both thought that we would want to cover the event. The guys name is Jason Kowalski."

"Max, why send me, I'm a sports writer, not a human interest writer. The paper would do better sending someone like that."

"The publisher said to send you, so, that's what I'm doing. Look it will be a chance to visit some of your old friends and family, you know, get acquainted with Chicago all over again. Besides when you wrote in Chicago, you did a lot of human interest type stories on personalities in sports, I read them they were good."

I sighed "there's nothing much I want from Chicago, not after everything I went through."

"I know, I know," Max waved me off. "You told all about that hundred's of times, but this is for the paper, you can't refuse us now." He looked at me with those sad bear like eyes that I didn't have the heart to say no.

That is how I ended up on a plane going into Midway airport. The paper didn't have the guts or the cash to get me on a larger airline. Thinking about everything on the way to Chicago left me with mixed feelings. I loved Chicago when things were going great for me there. Now, however, I just wanted to forget the past and get on with my life in Mesa. I got used to Mesa. It took me a while to get used to the summer and not having snow for Christmas. But once I got used to that I began to enjoy the place. It was laid back and although it had about 300, 000 people living there, it had a small town, laid-back atmosphere.

Landing at Midway, I picked up my rental car, a Ford Focus, no less. God is this paper cheap, and swung out onto the streets of Chicago and thought about my old neighborhood. It was eerie being in Chicago on assignment, something I hadn't done in years. After getting checked in at the hotel in the Loop (not one of the best, but at least it was in the heart of the city), I decided to rest and get ready to meet Kowalski later in the afternoon.

CHAPTER 2: THE FIRST MEETING

Believe it or not, Jason Kowalski, the subject of my story lived in Hegewhisch, near my old home. Talk about coming home again. The streets looked as they did when I was growing up. My parents had moved away a long time ago and both had passed away a few years ago. So, I thought while I was here, I might as well visit the old homestead for a couple of minutes.

The old home had a new paint job and some new windows, but looked pretty much the same as it did when I lived there. The kids on the streets played differently though.

When we played out on the streets, we played baseball, wiffleball actually, and touch football. Now, they were riding their skateboards or inline skates. Blame it on x-treme sports, I guess.

I couldn't ride a skateboard if my life depended on it. The one time I did (without my parents permission) I ended up dislocating my elbow. I spent the rest of the summer watching my friends play baseball and listening to rock music and a DJ named Dick Biondi.

Jason lived with his parents, in one of those two story bungalows in the Hegewisch section of Chicago. I wondered if he did the same things I did while growing up. Play baseball and football, ride bikes and maybe a little basketball now and then.

Taking another of those bumpy, curvy roads that connected my neighborhood to the rest of Chicago (the road that leads from nothingness to nowhere), I wondered what I would feel. Now, going through the area, nothing much had changed to rid me of that long ago concept.

There are no doorbells in Hegewisch; so, I knocked on the door. In a couple of minutes, the door opened and there stood Jason. "Hi there," he smiled, "I was expecting you, come on in."

Jason was not what I was expecting. He was about 33, I presume. He was short, about 5'7" and weighrd around 130 pounds. He was not a muscleman, but you could say wiry. Other than that, there was nothing remarkable about him. Actually seemed kind of shy. I thought, "this is going to be a long week," I thought I had better prepare myself for a tough sell, if I want the readers to have any type of connection with this guy.

Offering me a seat, he said that he had been told to expect me, but he thought that it would be more like tomorrow. "Maybe it's better this way." He laughed. "I would just be trying to figure out something to say. I'm not the type to do a lot of talking. I always figure that you learn more by listening than by talking all the time."

"Well, I thought that we should get together as soon as I got in. You know break the ice, and all. After all you'll be seeing me a lot this week."

"Really? I thought this was going to be a one shot thing, I didn't know the Cubs set it up for the whole time." He thought that he would just do his thing on one day in the next week and then be gone.

I told him that as I understood it, he was going to practice with the team as any player would do and then get a chance to play in one inning of one game. It was as if he was a player called up after the September 1 deadline. So that way there would be no league rule broken.

He let out a sigh and shook his head, then smiled in a crooked way. "Should have figured as much. I guess that's one way for the team to keep the team in the spotlight, what with the Sox doing so well this year.

I asked him why he's doing this. He shrugged and said "I was given a chance to fulfill a crazy dream, so I figured why not?"

He said that all he wanted was to gets some tickets to a game for a few friends that helped him and his family out when he was recovering from all the problems with the heart transplant. "There were so many people I wanted to show appreciation to for their support and I thought taking them all to a baseball game and watching my favorite team was the way to go," he said. Apparently, someone at the Cubs organization heard about his efforts and what his crazy dream was and convinced management to go along with the idea of having him play in one game toward the end of the season. "Maybe it was when I wrote Opra to see if I could get tickets, that the Cubs were notified," laughing at his audacity,

"The Sox had Minoso play when he was in his sixties and seventies, so, they figured why not?" Jason chuckled. "I said yes, but now that the time is near, I admit I'm a little scared."

But he did have a dream that he would play for the Cubs in a game. "Everybody has dreams, this is one of mine. Don't you have dreams, Mr. Sweeney?

I told him that I did, but I guess that in the intervening years that they have gotten lost or out of focus and I couldn't recall them as I once did. "Besides when you get to be an old dude as I am now, one trades warm fantasies for the cold realities of life.

It was getting late, and, I was tired. I told Kowalski I would pick him up the next day and go out to the ballpark. The Cubs were playing the last home stand for the year and Jason was invited to workout with the team this week before he got his chance to play.

"It will probably be a pinch running role," he said. "I doubt that they would put me on the field or bat." I never was that good a player, it's just that I love baseball and the Cubs, and, I figure that, at least once in your life, you should follow your instincts, if you get the chance.

Somehow, I think that I understand.


CHAPTER 3: DAY ONE

The next day, I got up earlier than usual. Called Max and told him that the first story would more than likely be ready by tomorrow. That I would fax it in using the hotels fax service. After breakfast I called Jason and arranged to pick him up around 10 am. I wanted to get a head start. I had not been to Wrigley Field in years and certainly wanted to make sure that management would welcome me when I arrived.

I called Jack Wesson, my liaison with the Cubs and set everything up, Then off I went. Jason was waiting outside when I arrived. His Mom called out just before he got in the car to make sure that he took his medication. "Are you on much?" I was concerned. But Jason replied. "I only take medication twice a day, at morning and at night, no problem."

Relieved I had a chance to take the measure of this guy called Kowalski. It seemed impossible that he could do anything on a baseball diamond. I told Jason that very thing. Jason shrugged his thin shoulders and said, " I have no illusions about any if this, but that is the beauty of it all. No one expects any thing from me, so, if I do good great, wonderful, if it turns into a dud, well, at least I tried."

Somehow again, I had to agree with Kowalski.

Despite my cynical attitude when I blew into town, I was beginning to like Kowalski. He had an enthusiasm for what he was about to do. Yet, he also was honest that he could be a laughing stock. Yet he was willing to soldier on and do what he wanted no matter what the odds.

Walking into Wrigley Field brought back a lot of memories, Surprisingly, many of them were when I was a kid. Being in my fifties I remembered how I used to watch games on my parents old back and white T.V. When my Dad took me to my first big league game at Wrigley, I was awed. The small, black and white picture exploded into a riot of size and color. The shades of gray turned into greens, white, red and blue. The midget baseball players grew into giants, as they should. They were so much more than anything I had seen before. The stories of Ruth, Banks, Aaron and Mantle grew in legend and stature before my eyes.

For Kowalski, it must have been even more exciting. Instead of being in the stands, he was going to play on the field; even it was just a half an inning. I never got the chance to even stand on the diamond in Wrigley Field as a kid. They didn't do that type of thing when I was growing up. Now Jason was going to have a chance to play. You could see he was nervous and very excited,

The Cub team, seemed to greet us with kindness and professionalism. The manager, the first baseman and their two top pitchers were especially kind. Considering that they were playing this game as their job, they were willing to help Jason feel comfortable in his new surroundings. They did the right things that would help to make a newcomer feel comfortable.

Yet, Jason wasn't that good, that was understood. He lacked the skills necessary to ever be a professional baseball player. He flubbed a few fly balls and he missed a lot pitches during batting practice. Yet he took it all in stride, never getting down on himself as he was doing something that he loved.  The practice was long and hard. The reward would come as the game started. Kowalski sat on the bench with the rest of the team. However tired he was, you could see he was having the time of his life.

After the practice, we stopped at a restaurant for dinner. For the first time, I had the opportunity to ask the question I had wanted to ask since I met Jason: why are you doing this? This is his story.

CHAPTER 4: JASON"S STORY PART 1

If you want to know why I'm doing this, let me tell you a little about myself. I never was a strong person, physically. I was born with a heart murmur that the doctor thought would disappear when I got older. I could do most things, only not as well as other kids that had a normal heart and health. I was always getting colds and the flu and I guess that has affected me even today. I always thought of myself as the weak kid on the block and I guess it showed.

But, what I couldn't do physically, I could do with my mind. My Mom taught me to read when I was four or five and by the time I was six, I was already reading the paper. Like my Mom always said," you might not be able to do much with your body, but develop your mind." So, that's what I did.

Having learned to read at an early age helped me tremendously. When I was in the first grade, I had already read the Dick and Jane books two years earlier. To me they were boring. I needed something more to read. The teachers would drool over my reading skills.

It probably looked like I was showing off in class with the way I could read. That didn't help me much with some of my classmates. They probably looked at me as what would be known today as being a nerd.

I love reading and still do a lot of intellectual stuff, history, art, music, politics, and writing. I also loved sports, even if I wasn't that good in it. Mostly though I loved baseball. Not that I didn't love other sports. It's just that baseball was something that I could do, at least a little. I didn't have to be a big person to play the game, and playing with the guys around the neighborhood was just fine with me.

All of us in the neighborhood played baseball from March through October. In the summertime, we would play 3 or 4 games or even more games a day. Whether it was the fields near our homes or on the diamond in the park. Everyone had a ball and bat and a glove. We ate and lived for the game. We used to have a field at the end of the block that was our baseball field. There we could play a little hard ball. Sometimes, we would play wiffle ball in the streets. But that was mostly when we were younger.

All of the guys thought of ourselves as the next Maris or Mantle or Aaron. I thought of myself as the next Ernie Banks, my favorite Cub player. I even held my bat in the same position as Banks, though I didn't have the wrist power that Ernie had.

When the weather was bad we would play some tabletop baseball game. So, the season never ended. All-star baseball, the game with the spinners and the round cards was our favorite game, on a rainy day we could play it forever.

When, we couldn't get together and play. We would play wall ball, just to keep our fielding skills intact. Sometimes we would play ten to fifteen games of wall ball a day. It seemed that summer was an endless baseball paradise in the neighborhood.

When I was ten, I finally convinced my parents to let me play Little League baseball. It seemed that the league that I wanted to join had a rule that everyone had to play in each game. I wanted top play on a Cub team, but I was placed on a team called the Yankees.

Coach Myers was a gruff kind of a guy, but his heart was in the right place. Obviously, he picked the really good players to start. I was always one of the last to take the field, in the last inning, usually in left field. That way I couldn't do much damage with the glove. I had stones for hands. My batting consisted of strike one, strike two, you're out.

That year we had a good team, especially the starters. We usually got a big lead, so when us scrubs had to take the field, the game was as good as won.

We got into the league championship. The team we were playing was called the Athletics. They had won the championship for the last four years. This year, we played them tough and were actually ahead in the game 5-4 with one inning left to go. Poor coach Myers, now he had to bring the scrubs in, including me. But so did the other team.

Coach looked at us and pleaded, "don't do anything to mess it up," We promised we wouldn't and promptly allowed two runs to score on a throwing error. Luckily, it was the right fielder that made the error, not me. We made it with out another run scoring, but now I had to bat in the bottom of the inning.

Johnny Miller walked; Harvey Jenkins flew out to the shortstop. Billy Stephens also walked. Josh Feinstein tapped out to the pitcher. That left me to come to the plate.

I was 0 for10 that summer, with 5 strikeouts. Their pitcher wasn't very good, but with my swing, it didn't matter.

Everyone on our team was moaning and saying that the game was as good as over. The Athletics were cheering thinking the game was in the bag. I couldn't have agreed more.

The first pitch was a ball, as was the next one. I was hoping I could walk my way on to first. The next pitch was a strike down the middle; I was determined to get the walk. The next pitch was another strike. I had better make my mind to swing; the walk strategy was not going to work.

Everyone was at a fever pitch. Coach Myers was in the dugout hands buried in his hands, he couldn't bear to watch.

I don't know what happened, but I swung at the next pitch, and somehow managed to hit it. The law of averages finally caught up with me. I was stunned, after standing there with my mouth open, I heard the screams of Coach Myers, "run you little bastard!"

The ball skimmed down the right field line, past the fielder and the two runs scored. We won the Championship. I was a hero.

Coach Myers was not allowed to coach the next year, because of his remark. But, it didn't matter. He had his championship; he could die a happy man.

As the summers came and went, we grew older and the days of playing baseball in the neighborhood started to come to an end. Some of the bigger boys on the block started to play organizes sports on their high school team. Some of them became pretty good. For me, the runt of the block at that time, I had to say goodbye to baseball as a sport I could play. My body couldn't keep up. I missed it, but I was glad for those summers that I had the chance to play.

Chapter 5: Day 2-ROB

The next day at Wrigley was one of those warm late September days. The sun felt good and for a while everyone could forget about the impending fall and winter. I was sitting in the stands, behind home plate, when Al Baker, my old assistant from my former Chicago paper came over to shake my hand and say hello.

"Rob, you old dog, what brings you back up this way?"

Al was my assistant for the last five years I worked at the paper in Chicago. Tall, gangly with a gap tooth smile, he would remind you of a country hick. But he was well educated. He worked his way through college as my assistant, going to the Northwestern School of Journalism. I knew that someday he would be a good reporter. When he took over my job on the paper, he did not fail me. He excelled in ways that I could not. He was well liked by all the players he interviewed. Always giving them a fair shake in the story and abiding by the rules of fairness in the world of journalism.

I smiled and said, "I'm here covering the kid who gets a chance to play ball with the Cubs. But, I hear you got my old position."

"Yeah, hey, I'm sorry about everything that happened. You got a raw deal, never wanted to get a job that way."

Al looked truly sorry. A young guy, he was thrust into a position that he would grow into pretty fast. He learned to roll with the punches in Chicago, a place that I thought was the second toughest town to write sports in, New York being the hardest.

"That's ok, I landed on my feet and got a nice job in Mesa, couldn't be happier." I don't know that it was a lie or not, but at that moment It leaned more
 toward the truth.

Al sat down and put his feet up on the sear in front of him, "How's the kid doing?"

"The manager said he's terrible, but, the kid doesn't seem to care, he's having the time of his life. Just look at him out there, does that look like someone who is worried about his job? I wish I could have that much fun with mine,"

"Will they let him play?" Al seemed genuinely concerned.

"Yeah," I said. That's the deal here, I'm sure that it won't be in a tight situation, probably as a pinch runner, couldn't see it any other way.

As Al and I continued to talk, I looked over at Jason. He did seem to be having the time of his life. He was eating up every moment that he was on the field. He couldn't run fast, could barely hit, and his fielding could be described as mediocre at best. He certainly was no Moonlight Graham, but like that fictional player; he was living a dream, his personal dream. I thought that this was all ridiculous when I was handed this assignment. Now, I wasn't so sure.

After practice, Jason would watch the game with me in the press box. I introduced him to many of my former colleagues. It was the first time I had seen many of them since I had left the paper. I had to admit I enjoyed it. This was my element. It was the time I enjoyed the most. The good times, the kidding, jokes and laughter in the press box was the best time of my life. During the game I asked Jason, what happened after that little league season?

CHAPTER 6: JASON'S STORY II

After, that little league season I didn't play for awhile but as I grew a little bit older I did get a bit stronger. By high school, I thought I was strong enough to play on our high school team and I tried out and made the freshman team that year. I practiced hard, almost every day, even in the winter, working out in the batting cage.

Yet, I couldn't get to that next level. Somehow, my heart problem kept me from really getting better. Then in my sophomore year I got some kind of virus that seemed to affect my heart. I was out of school for most of the year and when I tried to come back and play, the school wouldn't allow me to participate.

I wanted to play and be a part of the team, but coach could only offer me a chance to be equipment manager. So, I took it. At least I was part of game I loved. I would not have it any other way.

Also, I discovered music, and took up the guitar and became pretty good at it. I Still play today, even writing a little music.

You would think that would make me happy, and it does. Yet, in the back of my mind, I always wonder what could have been, if I could have played baseball and played in the big leagues.

Also, being disabled made me a little shy, especially around the girls. It wasn't that I never had a girlfriend but more often than not I didn't. I was always more a friend than anything else. Maybe it was my fault, I don't know. Maybe it was because I wasn't the jock type. I guess I felt a bit inferior, as stupid as that might be. I guess I didn't have what today would be called a good body image. Well, if I made a mistake in thinking that way, it's my fault and I'll have to live with it and move on.

I did pretty well in high school, not in the top ten, but in the top one hundred. Then I entered college, I went a state university that wasn't too far from home. That's where I met Gail. She was blond, shorter than I was (I'm not that tall), and seemed to be an open person. She went to school and volunteered her time at a nursing home entertaining the old folks with her saxophone.

At that time I was working with a group of disabled individuals called Handicapped Awareness. It was a natural for me. The people were open and warm and I made a lot of friends there. So, besides studying I was spending a great amount of time there. I soon became the de facto leader within the group. The two brothers that had set up the group still ran things but often they would ask for my input.

Ron and Jack were the opposite of each other. Ron was the elder brother. More analytical then Jack, he always tried to think of both sides of an issue to get the best solution to the problem.

I remember one evening when Ron and I were called over to o mutual friends house to help someone who was having a problem. After discovering that the problem was that a member of the group had gone out and had too much to drink and was pretty much passed out on the floor of our friends house, Ron asked "what our priorities?" Just like Ron, to want to analyze the problem before acting. But his heart was always in the right place. He was always thinking and dreaming and eventually did all right for himself in the last ten years or so.

His brother Jack was the complete opposite. Impulsive and sometimes reckless, he had the drive to live more by the seat of his pants than stepping to the beat of another's drum. He often argued with Ron on how the Handicapped Awareness group was to be run.

Often, in those arguments would find me in the middle. Literally looking from one side to the other as each brother grabbed my arm to emphasize their points. A lot of times I could see both sides of the argument, so I would take a little from each side and mold a solution together. What seemed to be a totally original idea was really the best of both plans that they had proposed. If they had stopped and figured it out, they wouldn't have needed me. But then again I wouldn't have had the opportunity I had in the group and there would be no story.

Jack unfortunately had Hodgkin's disease that eventually killed him. While all of us may have been frustrated with his impetuousness and erratic behavior at times, I would say that the group became a little more boring with out his presence.

But this was supposed to be about Gail and how I met her. Usually after our Handicapped Awareness meetings some of us would meet for coffee at a local restaurant. Gail would come in with a few of her friends after one of her classes for the same reason.

One evening she came over to sit with us. I think she had the 'hots' for Ron but I don't think Ron noticed. I certainly did though.

I was sitting next to her and had a nice long chat trying to find out more of who she was. Normally, I'm pretty quiet around girls and don't try to insinuate myself much. A defense mechanism, I guess. You can't get hurt if you don't make an effort and put out your hand, right?

So, anyway, we talked. She told me what she was going to school for. She wanted to be an occupational therapist and she told me about the saxophone playing at the retirement home.

That night I began thinking that she would not only be someone who would fit in well with the group but someone that I could possibly date. Before I could ask her out I needed a line or an excuse to get her to go out with me.

So I decided to call her up. I remembered that she said she lived in dorm that had a name with 'oak' in it. Now there were a number of dorms with oak as part of their name. The only thing I could do is to call every one of those dorms and find her. That's what I did. As usually happens, it was the last dorm on my list.

When I got the right dorm I had to get to the right floor. Luckily, I remembered the floor. Someone answered the phone and I asked for Gail. The person on the phone asked me which one? Now I knew her first name, but not her last. I told the person "The little blond haired girl, with glasses. Luckily for me that described Gail, she answered the phone.

Then I got into my spiel. I told her how I thought her background and personality would be a plus for the handicapped awareness group and that she would be a perfect fit to be a part of such a fine organization.

I didn't know if she bought my line, but the next week after our regular meeting I found her there like if she was waiting for me. Some of the group planned to go out that evening to see a movie that one of the dorms were showing and I invited her to join us. We went to see 'An Officer and a Gentleman,' a somewhat romantic type movie. Before the movie was half over I had managed to be holding hands with Gail and when we left with the others, the impression was that we had been going out for quite a while. I asked her out for the following week and she accepted.

I guess from the first date we became joined at the hip. Most of the first time out was spent in lip lock. You could easily say that from the time we first met we seemed to be made for each other. For me, it was a beautiful time. Gail was smart and funny, although a little bit of a smart mouth at times. But we all have some imperfections. Then again, I also can be a bit sarcastic at times. She seemed to understand my health problems. I learned a lot from her. So, I was comfortable with her and enjoyed her company.

After a few months, however, there were times I wasn't so sure. It seemed that there were times that she needed to get away and not want to be with me. One time we broke up for around 3 months. I was not happy about it. Friends could tell.

I'm not the type to express myself well and be open about what is going on in my life. It's just a Kowalski trait, as my sister once said. Gail was not the type to be open either, so that really was a problem for us. Neither of us could express what we were feeling at one time or another. I guess we were a challenge to each other.

I remember when we got back together for the first time, after the break up. I had to go to a friends wedding, afterward, instead of going to my place, I visited an old friend and stayed over night. When I got up early that morning, I decided to go to the church, where we both attended. I got there, tuxedo and all just around the time Mass was supposed to start. I sat in the front row. Gail was doing the readings. When she looked up to begin, there was no way she could have missed noticing me. Her head went back as if someone hit her with a rock. It was a total surprise.

When I went to communion, the priest, whom I knew, was about as taken back as Gail. Instead of saying "The body of Christ," as they do on presenting the host. He said "The body of Christ?" I guess he was wondering what was going on. I was wondering, myself. I wondered what Gail would say after Mass.

After Mass. Gail came up to me and asked what I was doing there. I was honest with her, as I always tried to be. "I'm thought I'd come and see if you wanted to have breakfast." She said "sure, but I got to tell someone, I can't make it with them,"

Then, I saw her go over to this other guy. I guess it was my competition. Anyway, she must have told him that she was going back with me. He didn't seem too happy, but what can I say. Some guys have it and some don't. This was one time that I had it. In fact, it was the only time.

Besides Gail and the Handicapped Group, I was president of the College History Club. Mostly, I was president because no one else wanted the job. It sounds like it was a pretty intellectual kind of club, but believe me it wasn't. We tried but since we were a small college, we never got much funding from the college, so we were pretty much on our own. Still we had a lot of fun.

One of my friends in the club was Cassidy, whom every one called Butch. They knew him as Butch Cassidy. People who knew that we hung out together would sometimes refer to me as Sundance. So we became the modern Butch Cassidy and the Sundance Kid.

Like I said our group took things a little less seriously than one would think. I remember one meeting where the discussion was whether to go to a cemetery where a number of Civil War dead were buried as well as other famous Illinois individuals. The alternative was to go to Moose Cholak's Wrestling Hall of Fame.

I knew Butch and a couple of others were just kidding me, but a few other members were rather upset that any money that we had would go to a trip like that. For my self I thought it was hilarious. In some ways I would have preferred the Wrestling Hall of Fame.

One trip that was the best was the trip we took to the Tippecanoe Battle Field, the site of a famous War of 1812 battle. We had separated into three cars and took off for the two-hour car ride down to the site. After visiting the Battlefield and enjoying the beautiful fall colors of the trees. We headed back home.

One of the cars was being driven by a few of the group who were more or less born again Christian. Now, I have nothing against anybody with how they wish to believe. But one of the members of the group, whom we called Tuna, was our resident socialist. Being that way he had a bias against the born again types. On the way back, he came to us and asked if he could come with us in the pagan car. I suppose that was because we were listening to Beatles music and singing on the way down.

Like I said college was fun. It may be a drag for the first couple of years, but the last two years flew by fast and I can say it was one of the best experiences that I ever had.

CAHPTER 7: DAY 3: ROB

We got back late that evening. I had dinner at Jason's house, with his Mom and other relatives. They were delightful hosts and the dinner was simple but ample. During the evening they recounted how Jason finally started to go down hill. Slowly, he was getting weaker and weaker.

His mother wondered how long Jason could keep up the

pace that he had set for himself. "Eventually, I knew that something had to give, he was wearing himself out and it wouldn't be long until he would completely break down."

I wondered, "is that true, Jason?" He just laughed and said that "Sure, I knew it, but, I always felt that I would have plenty of time." I was the type that felt that if I die doing something I like, at least I'd die with a smile on my face. Actually, I held out longer than I thought I would."

Later I got back to the hotel and sat down at the laptop and wrote my second story:

TRANSPLANT KID READY FOR ACTION
By Rob Sweeney


Chicago-_Jason Kowalski, is ready to play, even if the Cubs are not sure yet.

After practicing with the team for the last two days, Kowalski says he's ready any time to play ball with his favorite team, The Chicago Cubs.

However, the Cubs manager, while impressed with the enthusiasm that Jason projects, is hesitant to play him just yet.

"We got to make sure he is ready," he said. "I know it's only a one shot, one inning deal, but I don't want to have him get hurt." The manager also commented that, with the Cubs, still in the division race, he has to make sure that the use of Kowalski, would not hurt his team's chances as far as the division race goes.

Kowalski understood. "I can see how important it is for everything to work out right. But man, I really can't wait to get out there!"

Other members of the Cubs are impressed with the

enthusiasm that Jason displayed. Many hopes that the enthusiasm and desire to play will rub off on them, as they get ready in the stretch run taking place now.

It can only be hoped that after Jason is gone, his desire to play this child's game will continue to be a standard for the Cubs and the rest of baseball.

It will be an interesting experiment. With the Cubs vying for a play-off spot, they can't afford any foul ups. It is a hope that Jason will get his chance to play and the Cubs get their chance to get to the World Series. Both seem like impossible odds.

--------------------------------------------------------------------------------

After writing my article, I sent to the newspaper as an attachment for an E-mail.

With my work for the day finished, I went to sleep.

CHAPTER 8: ROB

With the Cubs playing an evening game, I had a whole morning to kill. I decided to visit my old newspaper office and see what was going on there. I wondered how I would be accepted, as an outcast? Or would I be considered a hero? After five years, I even wondered if anyone really cared. Well, I guess I'll find out.

Coming into the Loop is still a startling experience. Now, Phoenix is big and growing all the time. There are traffic tie-ups on U. S. 10. But compared to Chicago, they're still minor. Chicago is still the City of Big Shoulders. It is still perceived as known as Gangster Town, in many parts of the world. The Dan Ryan, the main expressway is known as the Death Race 500. It is a crowded piece of work, made no less tolerable for the amount of construction that takes place in the summer.

In Chicago there are two seasons, it is said, winter and construction season. This summer the construction season was particularly bad. Some of the streets in the Loop were also getting a face-lift.

To me, it is still an exciting city, but, less so than before. After being in Mesa, I had become more laid back. The hustle and bustle of Chicago is no longer was a part of me. I even wondered how I managed to survive, before all the trouble and the move to Mesa.

Even Phoenix, Arizona and it's downtown seems quiet compared to Chicago. The first time I entered downtown Phoenix was a study in amazement. It was a little noisy and confusing, but not near like Chicago. It was almost a relaxing stroll, compared to the Loop.

The offices were next to the Chicago River. It is a murky gray river, the only time it looks alive is around St. Patrick's Day. That's when Mayor Daley and his political army dye the river green, to the delight and chagrin' of the Chicago faithful. Then again Ritchie Daley is a Sox fan, so I have to forgive him. Sox fans seem to do the strangest things.

The city desk looked much the same, only a bit quieter. With the onset of computers, you no longer heard the clack of typewriters. More and more use is made of the Internet. Stories are not called in, but faxed. Even the printing process is quieter. Type is set by computer and programs run the office, not the reporters or editor any more.

The first to greet me was Al. "look here, the prodigal son, returns!"

"Shut up and get back to work." I was amazed how I fell back to the same old routine. Most of the old staff was there, although Ed Larson retired a few months ago, and Chris Wilson died a couple of years back.

Jim Hudson, the sports editor for the paper, came over to

greet me. Jim and I never got along that well. Younger than I, he acted more like a publisher than an editor. To me, he always seemed interested in getting publicity for the paper than making sure stories were accurate and timely. I guess I come from the old school of journalism, where no one played fast and loose with facts.

Shaking my hand, I could see that he had suspicions on my motives. He also had some news to tell me.

Handing me some hard copy Jim said, "Looks like your story is causing some waves, the commissioners office is denying that they gave the Cubs permission to use your kid for the game."

The hard copy read: "The Commissioner of Major League Baseball is requesting that the Cubs Organization, to disallow Jason Kowalski to partake in any kind of activity with the baseball team until it can be established that all issues concerning his playing for the team can be clarified."

Al said, "Your story is being picked up all over, including our paper. Apparently, Major League Baseball got caught with its pants down and didn't realize what the Cubs were doing.

"Impossible." I said. "I got reassurances that everything was on the up and up."

"Well, I think some one is fooling some one," Jim looked like he was enjoying this, just like he enjoyed my demise from the paper five years earlier.

With that the visit was ended. I rushed back to my car and sped off to Wrigley Field to talk with some top brass and see what the heck was happening.

They assured me at Wrigley that, yes, there was a snag, but the mix up was to be taken care of promptly. That in the end, nothing will change.

I decided to go to Kowalski's house and see what he was thinking. On the way over, I turned on the radio and listened to one of the sports talk shows. My story about Jason was the only topic of discussion. And it was mixed.

1st caller: Hey, if the kid wants to play and the Cubs are stupid enough to let him, then let him play.

2nd caller: Mr. Kowalski is not very good, I hear. He'll just embarrass himself or worse yet, hurt himself. They shouldn't do it.

Announcer: the integrity of Baseball is at stake. If we do this, the sport will be no better than professional wrestling,

And on it went. Spending my time with Jason and his family, I had not kept up with the news. It seemed that everyone was getting on the bandwagon. The networks, the sports channels, CNN, MSNBC, FOX NEWS, all of them were putting their two cents in Even Bill O' Reilly made the subject part of his talking points. I had never had a story that made so many people notice, ever.

Suddenly I had become a celebrity again. I used to have a syndicated column before I was fired. But in the intervening five years I was not heard from. Again it was a story where my integrity was at stake, if it felt like Déjà vu all over again, it was.

At Kowalski's house, reporters had set up camp. I had to park about two blocks away and walk over to his place. Reporters swarmed me; the flash of the photographer's camera was constant.

"What do you think of all of this?"

"Can the kid play?"

"Do you agree with the Commissioner?" And so on….

All I could answer was "No comment" to each question. I pushed my way to the front door and with the help of Jason's uncle, squeezed in.

Jason was sitting on the front couch. He looked as shell shocked as I was. I apologized for what had now happened. He said that there was nothing to be sorry about. "If not you, someone else would have written the story and I would still be in all of this, anyway. The most important thing is to get to the bottom of the problem and straighten it out.

I couldn't help thinking he was right. If not me, there would be someone else. There's always someone who would be after the story. It's the nature of the game these days. The press was always ready to build you up then tear you down; I had seen it so many times before. It had even happened to me.

Yet, I had to wonder. Was I right for this story? How did I feel about what Kowalski was doing? Was what he was doing worth it?

I had to admit that up until now I treated the story with an air of objectivity, not really caring about why Jason was doing or if he was doing the right thing. I knew that I had to help him, but whom was I doing it for? Was it for me or was it for him? I didn't have an answer. I would have to wait for the enlightenment, later.

The first thing was getting Jason out of the house. We decided to go out the back way and hoof it to my car, before the press found out. It would be risky, but the chance for success was good for this time, anyway.

His Uncle Sam would go out and make a short statement to the media outside. While he was making his statement, we would sneak out. "Make sure, it at least five minutes long," I said. "That way, all the attention will be focused on you and we can make a break, that should give us enough time to get to the car and away."

As Uncle Sam came out to speak, we made a hasty escape out the back door and through the alley. Without anyone noticing, we made it to my car and onto Lake Shore Drive to Wrigley Field.

Once at Wrigley Jason and I immediately barged into the Managers office. The manager was not too happy to see us, but reluctantly let us in. "I'm sorry about this Jason, but I have no choice but to obey the order of the Commissioner. The Commissioner has scheduled a hearing on the matter for two days from now. A representative from the Cubs will be with you for the meeting and you can bring anyone else with you.

Kowalski didn't bat an eye. "I'd like Mr. Sweeney to also come with me." He turned to me and said, "Can you do it?"

Now was my turn to make a decision. Do I stay on the sideline, or do I follow the story through to the end? I decided to follow the story, or should I say the man, right to the end. One thing I knew, I was a reporter. "Sure, I'll go."

"Good," said the manager. "Don't practice tonight, but there is no law that says you can't be in the dugout. Just don't put on the uniform. Tomorrow you'll head for New York."

As we went through the clubhouse, other members of the Cubs expressed their support for Jason and wished him good luck in his quest to play.

Reporters were there, also. I told Jason that he did not have to talk with them. However, Jason decided that he should make some kind of a statement and asked if I would help him compose it.

After a few minutes a statement was put together and

Kowalski went out to speak with the press for the first time. The statement said:

"As you know I was invited to play baseball with the Chicago Cubs for one inning of a baseball game. In part to fulfill a dream that I always had to play professional baseball and play for my favorite team, the Chicago Cubs. Due to a heart problem, I was never able to play baseball or carry out the dream of playing professional baseball.

Two years ago, I received a heart transplant and after three years, two of which was spent in intense physical therapy, I have reached some measure of health. I will never have the complete health or body of some of these athletes around me. Yet, through the kindness of people who know me and the kindness of the Cubs organization, I have been offered a chance to live my dream in some small way.

Today, Major League Baseball has decided that before I can participate, they wish to speak with me and to a representative of the Cub organization, to determine whether it is appropriate for me do play. That meeting will take place in the next couple of days.

At that time, I look forward to answering their questions and have the opportunity to achieve my dream. With that in mind I will not practice or play until that decision is made. If the decision goes against me, I will not play and I will thank the Cub organization for their willingness to go along with this dream. If I am allowed to play, I will do my best not to embarrass the Cub organization or myself. Thank you for your time and patience."

With that the meeting with the press was over. We walked back into the locker room and got ready to sit in the dugout and watch the game. Later we would arrange the flight the Cub representative and prepare for the meeting In New York and the Commissioner.

After the game we met with the Cub representative, a lawyer named Tim Gavin. He had asked to be our representative in part because he had known a number of people who were disabled and who wanted to either work or participate in an activity and were denied. He had helped others before and he wanted to help now.

Tim was tall and had his body seemed to be loose jointed and composed of angles. He was one of a group of lawyers called Gavin and Associates, which was originally founded by his father. Despite his apparent wealth, he was involved with a number of charity organizations, one of which was a halfway house for recovering drug addicts. He was the type of person I later found out that would give you the shirt off his back as long as you made an honest effort to improve you life.

Sympathetic to our problem, he cautioned us to the difficulties that lay ahead. "You have to understand," he said, "the Commissioner and Baseball is very protective of its image of promoting athletes that are strong and worthy of the game. It doesn't like to be fooled or interfered with. You are considered a "problem" to them that must be addressed.

"Is that why they have a steroid problem?" I countered. "It seems to me that if they cannot control that problem, they have no right in trying to dictate their view in this matter."

Gavin shrugged. "You may have a point, but we have to deal with the realities here. The concern is how do we get them to approve this person to play baseball and not tell them how to get their house in order."

It was important that Jason state his case in a clear, energetic manner. We both looked at Jason and he looked at us and said, "I suppose it is up to me, I'll have to do the best I can."

With that we decided to meet tomorrow on the plane and get

ready for the meeting in New York.

CHAPTER 9: ON TO NEW YORK

Tim, Jason and I met at O'Hare airport for a flight to New York. Before I left the hotel I e-mailed another story to my paper for publication:

---

KOWALSKI TO MEET WITH COMMISSIONER

Chicago_ Jason Kowalski is involved in something that is becoming more a nightmare than a dream. A heart transplant patient, Kowalski hoped to play an inning of professional baseball with the Chicago Cubs by the end of the week.

Instead, he is to meet with the Commissioner of baseball to resolve his status, due to concerns that his taking the field would be detrimental to baseball and himself.

In a statement to the press, Jason acknowledged the problems, and stood by the call to meet with the Commissioner and resolve any concerns that he may have. He also indicated that he would abide by any decision that is made.

I will be going with Jason as a representative and will continue to report on this developing story there. It is hoped that at this meeting the concerns that the Commissioner will be addressed and Mr. Kowalski will be able to achieve his dream of playing professional baseball.

---

Reading the story at the airport, Kowalski was grateful for the tone of my article. He felt that the opinions he had heard over the last few days were disguised as reporting. "It seems that everyone has an opinion of what the heck I'm doing, without seeing what the facts are. They don't even know my motivation."

"That's how the press works, these days," I countered. "Today facts are opinions and opinions are facts. We don't try to be objective and let the facts speak for themselves. These days, it's what I call creative journalism. It's bending the facts to support your opinion. We refuse to let facts stand for themselves and draw our opinions on what the reality is.

Tim Gavin laughed. "Rob, you'll never make a good lawyer. That's how cases are won in court. Now, what you describe would make you a competent historian, but a lawyer, never."

He explained that in court these days, it mattered more on how you colored the facts that you had rather than letting the facts speak for themselves. In this way a lawyer was more of an advocate than a seeker of truth.

I could only agree. In my more philosophical moments, I often thought that I would have rather been a historian, not a journalist. But life has a way of sneaking up on you.

Getting on the plane, I asked that I sit with Jason to continue to talk with him on what led to his desire to play baseball, even if it only was one inning. Tim said fine, there was little we can do until we reached New York. So, I sat next to Jason and told him to just talk about anything that he wanted to. Perhaps, then I could understand more of his motivations and his dream. We got our drinks, and Jason began to talk.

CHAPTER 10: JASON'S STORY CONTINUED

Let's see. I guess that I should finish up with Gail before anything else. We stayed together for neatly 3 years. For most of that time it was idyllic. We went out got to meet our mutual friends, went out to movies, sport events and just spent some quiet times at each other's place.

Still there were times that I wasn't sure that Gail was happy. There were times that I felt that she was still here mostly because was there was nothing else to do. Neither of us wanted to make a move to resolve whatever was the problem.

Since, I was working at a warehouse, and finishing school, I certainly thought that I would want to marry someday and I couldn't find someone as good as Gail to share life's journey with.

So one day late on a late summer evening, I told Gail that we needed to talk. I asked her what she felt about me because I know that someday I would want to marry her and I wanted to know what she felt about that.

I could see that she was in some pain. She said, "Sure I thought about that. But I also think that you may get weaker than what you are now, I wonder if you can have the energy to take care of a family. What if we have a bunch of little Jason's in the back of our car? What if you die? I'll be the one left to take care of them. I don't always know if I can deal with that."

Well, I was hoping for a different answer, but, I wanted honesty and I got it. I could have given a number of answers. I could have said that except for the grace of God you and I. I could have said that any time the roles could be reversed. It is just a twist of fate that it's me with the health problem.

I could have put my arms around her and said that we could work through it and I would stick it out until she feels better about her for me and our future.

That's what I wanted to do, but I didn't. To this day, I don't know why.

There were a lot of things that I could have said. I could have said that for the Grace of God go I. That if the shoe were on the other foot I wouldn't have hesitated to stand by her side and see it through with her.

I could have said that anything could happen any time. She could walk out on the street tomorrow and be hit by a car and I would be left alone.

I could recover one day or maybe there would be a miracle cure.

But if I said all of that, would it have made any difference? I think not.

Instead, I decided that if she felt that uneasy about our relationship, perhaps we should not continue. A couple of days after out talk, I told her so. It was hard for both of us, I'm sure. I could see it in her voice and manner as we talked or saw each other in the next few months. We had mutual friends, so it was hard not to run into each other. There was a few times that I thought we would get together, but I stood my ground, no matter how much it broke my heart. Or hers.

In the end, I believe she was right. Given what happened in later years. I sometimes wish I could see her and show her that I survived. Not to show her up but to share how well I am now.

I often wonder how she is doing now. I know she married and has at least one child. But after a few years, we had fewer and fewer mutual friends. So in the last couple of years I only had a memory and sometimes it doesn't feel enough to keep one warm at night. But I've managed to survive to the best of my ability.

If you ask me do I still think about her, I would say not much, just every God damn day.

There were other girlfriends after Gail, but some how it wasn't quite the same.

One girlfriend was one I also knew in college. When I met her I was out of school and she worked as a clerk in the county tax office, we got to talk and I asked her out. We had a pretty good time till one time when we went to a picnic for the fourth of July. The fireworks were great and we were awed at the display. After the picnic we got to talk about parents and she expressed her contempt and anger for he father. Now I understand that sometimes we can have issues with our parents, but really hate them?

Also, I thought, "this girl is looking for a father, I don't mind being a boyfriend, that's hard enough, but I don't want to be a father, too." I guess both of us knew that it wouldn't work out. Eventually we just stopped seeing each other.

Another time friends from work fixed me up with this one girl. She seemed nice, but a little bossy. Later that evening, I found out why. She was once a sergeant in the army! Now, I'm tolerant of military types, but I'm a little uncomfortable when they bring their military attitudes to a dating situation. Besides I'm your basic pacifist. I'm uncomfortable with guns and I'm not the type that would ever be able to abide that type of discipline. So, you guessed it. The situation ended.

Another gal I went with for a while was fine, except that she couldn't see being serious unless the guy made a certain amount of money. Well, considering that I knew that I would never make gobs of money. That would not work, maybe it could have worked, but after the disappointment with Gail I wasn't going to go through that again. At least we have remained friends.

After a few years of situations like that, I guess I was tired of playing the game. Eventually, I just stopped looking. I was happy with myself, and if I had to conform to someone's standard. I'd rather not.

Maybe it was a mistake. But as I see it, after and everything that I went through, as I got older, I think I made the right decisions.

Yes, it has not been easy. Sometimes I feel like that line from a Beach Boys song: "So herd to lift the jeweled scepter when the weight turns a smile to a frown." But I did survive with my integrity intact. There are times I wonder if it's enough.

But I see that they say were about to land in New York. When we settle in, I can tell you more.

CHAPTER 11: IN NEW YORK-ROB

We arrived in New York on a windy, rainy day. It sort of fit my mood. I thought that all of this was ridiculous, If someone wanted to something, as long as it was understood that it might be a problem for them and wasn't a problem for others, then they should be able to fulfill their dreams. It occurred to me that I was crossing the line as a reporter. I was no longer just a witness. I had become a participant. Yet, I didn't care. Sometimes one had to leave the sidelines and become part of the story. It was true here. It was also true of life.

At the airport, there was the same amount of reporters as there was in Chicago. The story had become national in scope. Again, Jason, Tim and myself had to make a decision. Whether we wanted to talk to the news people or to avoid them.

Jason decided to face them head on. "I appreciate the interest that my story has caused, but to keep the hearing as free from conflict as possible, I wish to refrain from making any statement at this time." At that point, we picked up our bags and walked to our waiting rental car.

The press was stunned. They were hungry for a story, a quote, anything. Instead they were reduced to running behind us and grasping for any sliver of controversy that would fuel their appetite and those of each of their respective media.

New York is a city that does not impress me. It is noisy,

nosey and grimy. I guess being in and working in Chicago for many years. I should be used to like the hustle of a big city, but not anymore. That's not to say that the city does not have a certain character, which is different from Chicago. Yet, having been in Mesa and the Southwest I have less interest in the large cities than I had before. No doubt I had become a Mesa man and a true citizen of Arizona.

When we arrived at the hotel, Tim called the Commissioners office and after a period of time came to my room where Jason and I were watching T.V.

"They set the meeting for 10 am tomorrow." Tim announced. "I think it will be a long, thorough meeting that will resolve our concerns, one way or the other. I hope that we can convince them. It might be a battle."

"Do we have a chance?" I asked. "What can we present as evidence?"

Tim smiled wanly. "Our best evidence is Jason. We can present the entire doctor reports and other type of evidence that shows that Jason is not a clear and present danger, to himself and the others in the field. But, the best evidence is Jason's determination to fulfill his dream.

Jason readily agreed. "This is about me. I'm the one that has to convince the Commissioner that doing this is not only a good thing for me, but also good for baseball".

All of us decided to go out for lunch. I knew a small out of the way place that I had visited a number of times when I had come to New York over the years. When we entered the diner (Italian, of course) Jason looked around and chuckled. "This looks something out of the Godfather. All I need to do is look around and I'll see Michael Corleone sitting at one of the tables waiting to make a hit."

I had to agree. "I always thought that this place a character.

Of course I thought it had more of a flavor of a Billy Joel song."

Tim said. "You're both wrong, it reminds me more of the early Simon and Garfunkel songs."

I could only agree that all of us were right. Each of us was seeing something based on our own experiences and interpretations. In the end, that's how this case would be decided.

After a good Italian meal and sitting around with our wine (grape juice for Jason, his medication kept him from having alcohol), I asked Jason to continue with his story. Taking a sip, Jason closed his eyes and thought a minute. Then he said, "I suppose I should talk about my Illness and what happened just before I had the transplant."

CAHPTER 12; JASON'S STORY- THE INTERLUDE

Excuse me if at times I get a little emotional about things at this point. Certainly, the next four years were the most challenging that I ever had to experience. It was a challenge for my whole family. I wouldn't wish the experience on my worst enemy, which, I don't believe I have any.

As I said before, I was working in a warehouse that distributed medical supplies. It paid well enough and even though it wasn't in my chosen field, I had plenty of other activities to use some of the things I learned in College. My philosophy has always been that I make enough money to do the other things I wanted to do in life. So, that being the case I was happy.

As I continued working, I noticed that, more often than not, I was getting tired. I lost a little zip. I was not able to catch my breath as quickly as before. More and more I was a bit grabbier, less patient, than before. I was beginning to feel the effects of having a bad heart and it sometimes showed in how I dealt with people.

I never was one to suffer fools easily. It must be a family trait. Now, however, I tolerated fools less than before.

Dealing with home was just as hard. I had moved back home after college, in part to save money and to help my parents as my father was not well and I thought I could be of help.

Unfortunately, because I could do less and less, I felt more of a burden than help. I was most frustrated. I can admit I also became more withdrawn. I had my job, of course. I still worked with the handicapped group when I could. I had taken over the group by that time. But with fewer people able to help out, I had to disband the group. Slowly, the rest of life became less and less a joy. It was harder to be alive when the energy that you needed to live life to the utmost becomes less and less.

More and more I needed to rest. My days consisted of struggling to get up, hacking my way to work, struggling through another day at work, then coming home and trying to get enough rest to face the next day.

Finally, tired of being tired, I went to a specialist at the university of Chicago. Dr. Jamrose had developed a way of fixing a problem such as I had and I wanted to find out if there was a chance that he could do something for me.

Dr. Jamrose was a kindly type of guy. Short and round, he had, nevertheless an intelligent look about him and an honest manner. He examined me and after minced no words about what he thought.

"I really doubt that much can be done. But the best way for me to know would be to have you catheterized and then decide what would be the best way to go. I won't promise you anything. At least you will have some answers." Then he set up the date for the catheterization.

I set up some vacation time at work and figured that I would be out no more than eight weeks, if something would be done. Little did I know that it would be almost four years later before I would return to work.

With Dr, Kendall assisting, Dr. Jamrose performed the catherization in early September of that year. They tried all types of tests while they had me on the table. In the end, nothing could be done. There was no way to fix my problem.

The next morning, the doctors told me that eventually I would probably need a transplant as the only remedy. Since I was in good shape otherwise, they thought it would be successful and the best solution for me.

While I was not surprised (I only had a hope that this procedure would work, I understood it was a long shot), I was not expecting the next part.

"You ought to go on disability and not work." Dr Kendall said. "Working as you are now only puts more strain on your heart. I won't be that bad, my own father had to go on disability and you can look on it as early retirement"

Well, I can't say I was totally unhappy. I had been so tired on the job; I was looking forward to a little rest. I remember getting on the phone, when I got home and saying to the supervisor, "I have to go on disability, I'm out of here, and I'm history!"

Yes I was that glad to be out of there at that time.

And it was like retirement for the first few months. I got a lot of rest, visited friends, worked on my computer skills and even felt stronger than I felt in a month of Sundays.

I felt so good that I thought that the doctors were just kidding me. Like they were playing a joke on me. There were times that I felt so good that perhaps I should go back to work. There were times that I was bored. With everyone else working, I couldn't expect to go out all the time. You can only read and play on the computer only so much. Besides, when I felt good, I enjoyed being out and making my own money.

Yep, retirement is nice. But, unless you have something to do, it can be a little boring.

In late December of that year, I developed some difficulty breathing. I figured that it was one of my bouts with bronchitis, again. So I went to my general doctor, who agreed that it probably was bronchitis or an upper respiratory infection.

He gave me a breathing treatment and some medication and said that I should come back with in a week. I did feel somewhat better and was able to celebrate Christmas fairly well.

By New Years Eve, however, I was feeling pretty run down again, I slept most of New Years Day and felt slightly better. By January 3$^{rd}$, though, I could hardly catch a breath. I called a friend of mine and he took me to the hospital emergency room, where I was admitted.

I spent three days there. They tested and prodded, as all hospitals do. They gave me medication and an I.V. I thought I felt better and they did send me home after the third day.

I came home but the next day, I was feeling no better than I felt the first time. So back to the hospital I went.

This time I remained on oxygen full time. My Doctor came in and let me know what he thought I needed. I needed heart transplant. "If we don't do something soon, you will be pushing up daises."

The only thing I asked that we could find somewhere in the

Chicago area. Earlier it was suggested that I go to St. Louis for the testing and transplant. I had rejected that because of the distance from home, family and friends." Surely," I told my doctor, "there has to be some hospital in the area that would do the procedure. This is a big city and area. I can not believe that there is nothing around here."

My doctor assured me that it was possible and he would find out where. Meanwhile, I had to go home with 24hour oxygen.

Now that was an experience I was not expecting. The hospital set everything up and I went home to a technician who showed me how to work the oxygen concentrator that I would be hooked up to and how to care for the equipment and arranged for a portable system for when I went out.

It was strange to be dependent on a machine that would give me some comfort in living. It's also surprising to notice all the other people that use oxygen when before, you never noticed anyone before using oxygen.

You know, I often asked God why I had to go through all of this. I still do. Even today. My only way of justifying any of this experience is to observe that what God wants, God gets. That is a simpler way of saying we are here to do God's will.

But, I see it's getting late and we better get back to the hotel. I hope I didn't bore you.

CHAPTER 13: BACK AT THE HOTEL-ROB

After Jason's story, I could only wonder if I knew what the future held for me as Kowalski did, would I be willing to go on? I don't know if I could have had the same amount of patience. He really seemed to bear the trouble he had, with a certain amount of grace.

Telling Jason what I thought, he just shrugged and said, "I really had no choice. My Father was ill and I didn't want to be more of a burden then I had to be."

Tim walked into my room at that moment and said that he got a message from the Commissioners office the meeting would take place at 1pm, instead of 10 AM as originally thought, It was to be held at the headquarters of professional baseball. He also had a surprise. "A couple of people from the Cubs organization will be part of my presentation."

"Who?" I asked. He only said that it was a surprise and that we would be pleased. I had to leave it at that.

I turned on the television. Again, there were more opinions on what should be done concerning Jason. Some were supportive and some were opposed. I couldn't understand what the problem was. It was then that I realized how much I became involved in this story. I had truly crossed the line of being objective. To my surprise, I didn't care. The more that I heard Kowalski's story the more I believed in his dream.

Did I ever have any dreams? Once I did. Now as life rolled on, I had disregarded them. Throwing them off like so many unwanted items that cluttered everything up. I had no dreams. I was weary and tired. I needed something or someone to wake me up again, throwing a mirror on who I am and show me the road back to who I truly was. I was beginning to think that this story would be the mirror that I needed.

Now, I sit in a hotel room in New York City wondering if I had the strength to follow my dreams and make them my reality.

That evening I wrote another article:
-----------------------------------------------------------------------------
THE KID IS READY

New York—With the meeting between the Commissioners of baseball concerning his ability to play, Jason Kowalski seems ready to plead his case.

In a long interview with this reporter, Kowalski related how he became disabled and his reaction to those hard times.

While resigned to whatever decision comes about, he also seemed determined to defend his dream as valid and worthy of consideration. He spoke of his family and their support and how much they mean to them. He spoke of the good times he has had with friends and coworkers. He truly seemed appreciative of their support through his struggles.

It is hoped that the evidence presented at 1pm tomorrow will convince baseball and the Commissioner that one persons dream is reflective of the dreams that everyone has. That everyone should be able to live their dream at one time or another in their life. If Kowalski were denied his dream, then it would be fair to say that everyone's dream is not worthy of being lived out.

Here's hoping that the message gets out.

----------------------------------------------------------------------------

With the story written, I e-mailed it to the paper. I knew it wasn't the most objective story I had ever written, but I didn't care. I was in too deep to pretend that I was just another reporter delivering another story. I was more than that. I was part of the story.

CHAPTER 14: ROB AGAIN

Early the next morning I got a call from my editor. "What kind of story is that? You never have put yourself into your stories before."

"Sorry about that, chief, ", I joked, doing my best Maxwell Smart. "Seriously, though, "I'm already part of the story so, why not say so. I think that's being honest."

My editor just snorted. "I don't know how that will be received by the readers. Do you want me to print the story as written?

Or do you want to change it?"

"No. If you want to put any type of disclaimer on it, go right ahead. That's yours and the paper's decision. For me the story stands.

Well, I know you to be a pretty straight on guy, so I'll let it go. I don't know what the other editors might say, though. I might have to run by them. My editor did not seem that enthusiastic.

"Whatever you say, boss." With that I hung up. Still yawning, I sort of crawled out of bed and stumbled to the couch. I was thinking that this day would be important, not only for me, but also for Kowalski.

With the meeting with the commissioner, Kowalski's dream would be determined. For myself, it could be the end of this adventure (which in a way it had become), or the beginning of the adventure (seeing if Jason can play and how well, for that one inning). Either way, I had discovered a new person emerging, myself.

Before our meeting today, I wanted to have another talk with Jason and learn more about what he went through. I imagined a lot. Maybe I could learn something about myself in the process. Now, I realized how important this story had become to me.

I went down to the restaurant to have breakfast and found Jason just finishing his.

"I guess, I'm a little bit anxious, he said. "I never thought all of this would turn out this way. I never dreamed that anyone would want me to live out my dream. I never thought I would fight this hard for it, also. Maybe, I'm thinking too much."

I smiled. "No, you have a right to be anxious, who wouldn't when something they dream about suddenly becomes a reality. I would react the same way as you."

Tim joined us and asked, "big confab here? Or, can anyone join?"

I told Tim that unless he had some strategy to plan with us, I want to take Kowalski out to Central Park and continue our interview.

Gavin said "No I think I covered everything with Jason last night. In fact it might be good for the both of you to get away for a while. You know, relax talk and enjoy the morning; it looks like a great day. That's a great sign. The more relaxed the both of you are, the better it will be later. Just be back by noon.

'Will do" I replied. I told Jason if he were up to it we'd take the subway to Central Park and take a walk. "I don't think we'll be bothered by reporters. They'll be getting ready to cover the meeting this afternoon. So we should be safe.

Kowalski, agreed and after my breakfast, we caught the subway and ventured out to Central Park.

Central Park is still the one thing in New York that makes the city bearable. Once considered a haven for criminals, it has been cleaned up and is the place to be if you want to run, play catch, read, and go on a picnic or just talk. From the outskirts of the park you can see the panorama of New York. You can see the skyscrapers, and the expensive apartments like the Dakota, when John Lennon once lived and were he was killed. I remember being in New York when Lennon died. For me it was a part of my youth cut away. It would never to be pieced together any more. I stood there in the park with thousands of others paying our last respects to someone who made us laugh, cry and think. Now Kowalski is telling us his dream. Would it be like John Lennon or would he also say 'the dream is over.'

## CHAPTER 15: JASON CONTINUES HIS STORY

After I got home from the hospital the second time and became hooked up to the oxygen supply, I became even more isolated than before. Now to get anywhere I had to plan short trips and make sure when I did go out, make sure I had enough of oxygen to last the trip.

Doing things around the house became a real chore. It was difficult for me to do even a simple thing like taking a bath or making my bed. If I wanted to take a shower I had to do without oxygen, which by the end of the shower left me really bushed. I could take a bath with the oxygen. But, to do that was a hassle and not very fun.

Making my bed in the morning was also a hassle. I could do it in spurts, but had to rest after each spurt. What should have taken me 5 minutes to straighten out and to fix the sheets on the bed took me close to twenty minutes. Getting dressed was no laughing matter either. It took me a while to get it together every morning.

If I wanted to clean my rooms at home, I would need about half a day. Vacuuming took almost forty minutes. Dusting took a good hour. It took a good half an hour to clean the bathroom. I had to rest after each exertion for at least a few minutes and wanted to do all those things less and less as time went on.

I could still drive and go out. While the portable system I was using worked great, I felt and sounded like Darth Vader. Once, I had to get up and speak at a meeting and I apologized for the way I sounded. I t kept me alive and all, but, at that time I felt it more as an embarrassment than a help. I didn't always enjoy going out.

Then there were the tests I had to take to see if I can have a transplant. I fit the age bracket. But the doctors needed to see if I could survive the transplant and how well I would survive after the transplant. They do this with everyone. There are times it would seem that the 'outcome' is more important than giving hope to the patient. But, it can also be said that they are looking to make sure that the patient will benefit from such a drastic procedure. I guess it can be argued either way. It depends on your point of view.

Well, anyway, the testing took almost five months to go through. It was hard to get to the hospital and because I would be so tired after each round of tests. Finally, I got through them all. After meeting with the psychologist I was through.

In early September of that year, I got a call from Loyola and they said that they have accepted me for a transplant. With my ok they put me on the list and I was set to begin the long wait.

CHAPTER 16: MEETING WITH THE COMISIONER

At noon we were ready to meet with the Commissioner. As we walked into the headquarters, we were escorted into a large hall, where the hearing would take place. "I thought it was going to be a private meeting," I said.

Tim replied, " I took a chance and didn't say anything. They told me last night that for the meeting were going to let the media cover the event, since there was so much interest in the story."

"Wouldn't Jason be a little nervous, with the media listening in?" I thought that the whole idea of a public hearing to be a shifty trick to pull on Kowalski.

"Nonsense," Gavin replied. "I have watched Jason handle the press and the whole process pretty well. He will have no problem handling the way it is conducted. In fact I think any testimony he gives here will only strengthen his case and bring a groundswell of sympathy for his cause,"

I thought about it for a moment and I had to agree. Jason had handled everything thrown at him, so far. What I had seen was someone who valued his opportunity to live his dream. The more I thought about it, the more I understood exactly what Tim was talking about.

Both of us went over to Jason. Tim told him not to be nervous. "You have nothing to fear. Just handle this in the same way you handled the press in Chicago and at the airport. You did a bang up job there, you can do the same here."

Kowalski nodded, "I know what I want to say. I suppose I've practiced it about a hundred times. I'm more worried about the all the legal stuff. After all I'm not up on everything as far as the rules of baseball and all the contract stuff."

"Don't worry about that. This hearing will hinge on the emotional aspect of your appeal. Once the crowd hears your story, they can't possibly say no. It's not like you're going to ruin baseball." Tim was sure on that.

I looked around at the crowd settling in. Off in the back rows I thought I noticed a couple of present and former Cub players. I turned to Tim and pointed, "Is that your surprise?"

Tim again smiled. "Yeah, I thought the best way to handle this was too throw everything at them. Create such an outcry of injustice that the Commissioner would have no choice but to drop his objections."

Jason laughed. "You're doing one of my things. When all else fails, throw in the kitchen sink!"

With that we made our way to the front of the hall and the table in front of the place the Commissioner and his staff would be seated.

Looking around, I thought the hearing looked more like a hearing before Congress, rather than a simple appeal to play baseball. I realized that my stories had generated a lot of interest. Maybe if I had not come down to Chicago earlier in the week, none of this would have been necessary. Jason could have played his one inning before the Commissioner would have known what hit him.

But then, there would have been someone or something that would have alerted the powers of baseball. Maybe my articles had caused a ground swell of support for Jason. Without the advance publicity, his chances to play and fulfill his dream would never have taken place.

All of this had to wait as the Commissioner and his staff walked in the room and took their places at the head table.

The commissioner spoke first. " Welcome to all of you here, and to you Mr. Kowalski, for coming to New York and meeting me here. I took the unprecedented step to have the meeting in an open forum because of the amount of interest the matter has generated. As all of you are aware there has been a lot of discussion since the stories, written by Mr. Sweeney first appeared.

There are those that say that, to allow someone who has had a serious operation, such as Mr. Kowalski has had should not even consider playing professional baseball, even for one inning.

There are some players that have said that to allow someone who has had a condition and a transplant like Kowalski makes a mockery of the sport of baseball.

I know that there are others who believe that to allow Kowalski to play shows the soft side of baseball. We all like underdogs, they say. We enjoy it when a team wins the World Series, either for the first time, like the Marlins or after a long period of time, like the Red Sox or the White Sox.

We enjoyed the play of Jimmy Piersal, who played with a mental handicap. His courage was portrayed in the movie 'Fear Strikes Out.'

We honor those who broke the color line in baseball, like Jackie Robinson. Their courage and talent are a source of pride for baseball."

The Commissioner continued. "However I also need to listen to those who say that we should never let those who have not played the game on a professional basis, let alone someone in Kowalski's condition to play the game of professional baseball. It does a disservice to the players. Why? Because they have spent many years and months to reach the point where they are now able to play the game, which they trained so long for.

It does a disservice to the fan, which pays good money to watch these well trained players in action, only to watch someone merely get by or even worse, not be able to play the game at all.

There are those that say that this type of gimmick sends a wrong message to the fan. That if you can soften an owner well enough, they'll let you play ball.

There have been older players, long past their prime that have been allowed to play ball. Minnie Minoso and Satchel Paige come to mind. But in both of those cases these were baseball greats who were allowed to play. They knew the game and the fans respected them.

Yes, there are many arguments, both pro and con, concerning this issue. While I would tend to be against this type of thing, I thought it would be better to discuss this openly and decisively. My only concern is for the integrity of the game of baseball."

With that the Commissioner finished his opening statement and allowed the testimony to begin.

So, there it was the argument for and against a mere fan that has a wish to play the game. I only wondered if Jason had the desire and the words to convince other after all that for this one time, he should get a chance to live his dream.

A number of owners had banded together to oppose the right of Kowalski to play. "It's preposterous," their spokesman shouted. : If we allow one owner to play a novice to play, what will have next? Will we have owners with bad teams getting these amateur types to play for less money? So they can cut their costs and make a profit?

One recently retired player was adamant about not letting Jason play. I have worked hard to play the game and done well at it. Now, someone who has hardly ever played wants to be in the same shoes that I once wore? Let him throw out the first ball and let the professionals play the game!

The chairman of the Players Association took a legalistic viewpoint. Would Kowalski be a part of the Players Union? Would he be paid as other baseball Players are paid? If not, then he is doing harm to the game. Baseball players have worked long and hard to get their rights. From Bill White on, we have worked to give the players what they felt they have deserved.

He continued. If, he is paid for his services as other baseball players, Kowalski would in effect demean everything that the baseball players have worked so hard for. If he plays for nothing, he does the same thing. Either way he hurts the player and ultimately every young athlete who also has dreams of playing baseball, if Mr. Kowalski wants to play baseball, let him play the game as part of the Transplant Games. That way he will be playing with a group of his peers. But don't do this as a major leaguer.

Other medical experts testified whether Jason should even have been practicing. "He has to be very careful", said one. "He could get some kind of an infection, which would be serious, given his compromised immune system. It is too dangerous to even think of doing what he is proposing. He should be happy to be alive and not try to do something that he has no business in doing."

Through all of this the crowd would cheer or moan, sometimes simultaneously depending on what side of the controversy they were on.

Jason sat mostly with a mask over his emotions. He figured that, eventually, He would get his chance to speak and tell everyone why he wanted this small Chance to play.

In the end the final judge would be the commissioner. He held to final say. On this matter and he had not decided yet.

Let me tell you a little about the Commissioner. He was a former executive of a major league baseball team. The owners had elected him in part because they felt he would look out more for their interests than of the players. A tall nerdy looking man, he had pretty much sided with the owners in most cases. Occasionally though, he would side with the players.

While the owners didn't like everything that he did, they would never get rid of him. Once, they got rid of a commissioner and for months did not hire a replacement and that the rest of the country screamed and yelled. They had to go back and hire a commissioner. When they did they hired the safest one they could find. Whoever heard of selecting someone to watch over you and they are the same as you?

The Commissioner had this big thing about the integrity of the game. Though it took the wrath of the United States Congress for Major League Baseball to pass stiff laws against steroids.

While the testimony was going on, Tim was in the back of the hall talking on his cell phone. After about an hour off and on the phone he came over to our table, all smiles. "I think I got us a way to pull us over the top." He said to me. "Remind me to thank your editor when this is all over."

I had one of those puzzled looks that I sometimes get when stumped working a crossword puzzle and can not figure out the word that I'm look for.

Gavin said. "Everyone will be heard from this time."

Somehow, the look on Gavin face said that we might still be in the game.

Now it was our turn. As agreed Tim Gavin would lead off first. Then I would be next. We felt that Jason should be last to speak. It would give us a chance to end with our strongest card. Then as Tim had said before, he would end our part of our argument. Tim also had his surprise. What it was I still didn't know, but before he began to speak to the assembled, including the Commissioner, he said to me, "If anyone from the postal service comes over to you while I'm speaking, just tell him or her to wait."

The audience quieted as Tim began to speak:

Commissioner, members of Major League Baseball, Player Union and other invited guests, I am happy to be here today to discuss with you the reason why I feel that Jason Kowalski should be allowed to play baseball for on day. I am Tim Gavin, representing the Chicago Cubs in the matter.

In researching the circumstances of this case, I have come to know Jason, not just as a client, but as a person, who has dreams and goal, as all of us have had, in our lives, at one time or another.

I have learned much about people who have had transplants and how they are able to lead strong, productive lives. Many have been able to go back to their professions and jobs they once have had before their transplants.

More important, these people are able to have dreams again. They have a desire to fulfill their drams and when ever possible, succeed in doing just that.

Such is the case of Jason Kowalski. Given a hard road to follow. He has never the less, survived, and even prospered in getting his life back on track,

Now, Jason would probably be the first to admit that it has not always been easy. There have been setbacks and downturns. Yet, he has found a way to overcome those obstacles and become a stronger person than what he was before.

Now let me answer some of the questions that have been asked here, today.

First, is Jason Kowalski able to play baseball? I don't know how good a baseball player he is (smiling as he says this). I do know however, that he should be able to play for the amount that he is being asked to. I present a report given to me by Dr, Garrison, and his doctor in charge of Mr. Kowalski at Loyola Medical Center.

In this report of Mr. Kowalski's it is reported that all his vitals are in the normal range and he has no problem with any of his medications he has been taking since receiving the transplant.

It is reported and Mr. Kowalski verifies that he has been

walking two miles a day over the last year. In addition, Mr. Kowalski has been building his upper body strength by using small weights. There should be no question here that he comes a long way in getting his general health up to the strongest point possible.

As far as not letting him play, because he is not in shape to play baseball. Did we say that to Minnie Minoso or Satchel Paige? Both were well past their primes, they both in part played because they were an attraction to fans that remembered them in earlier days when they had great command of their pitches and their bats.

We let Eddie Gaudel play for the St. Louis Brown in the 1940's. A midget that had no strike zone, baseball could have banned him and others before they ever set out on the diamond.

This is nor being done for publicity, but for kindness sake. It is a one shot deal. It is not a season long or even a weeklong tryout. If occasionally we do such things as this and don't always think we are ruining the great American Pastime, we are doing well.

There are so many other things in baseball that need to be addressed. We have a rampant steroid problem in the sport. We have the problem of revenue sharing and how to share the revenues so that small market teams can be competitive in an era of big money.

Yet, here is someone who loves the sport in a pure way. He loves it so much that he wants to play the game. Yet, we take the time to study this while larger problems are ignored or swept under the rug.

I thank you for allowing me to speak and hope you will take my comment in the correct way.

After Tim finished I could only whisper that he sure stole a lot of my thunder. I was next and after his statement I could only be described as a loss for words. I would have to start from scratch. I would have sometime because we were on a break

After the break, it was my turn to talk. Let me repeat what I finally said:

Let me wish a good day to all of you. My name is Rob Sweeney, I write for a paper in Mesa, Arizona. A little over a week ago, I was sent on assignment to cover the debut of Jason Kowalski as a baseball player for the Chicago Cubs.

Having worked in Chicago as a sports reporter for many years I was familiar with the city and the Cubs. I presume that is the reason for my assignment. I was the first to write about Jason and his dream of playing baseball. In part I am the reason why we are all here today.

I was reluctant to take on this assignment when it came up. I thought that it was a boring assignment that held little interest. However I as got to know Jason Kowalski, I have learned a lot about him, baseball and about myself. I am proud to call Jason a friend and am happy to write about his dream.

We all have dreams, some are small and some are big. We all want to accomplish something positive in this world in the time we have in it. Jason is no different than any one else in those dreams.

He has had a lot of obstacles in his way in achieving his dreams. Most are not of his making. Yet, he continues to persevere. To place one more obstacle in his quest of his dream would be wrong. Why?

I see baseball as losing its heart. I love the sport. It is the sport of my youth and a part of many boys' dreams. Today, it has become big business. The owners and cities want to have the best and spend millions of dollars: whether it is for the stadiums or the players.

Now here is a guy with a simple dream. He would love to play baseball. One day he is given a chance to play. Like any one else that has an opportunity to live his dream, he says yes. Who are we to deny it? If we deny this to him, we say that those who are deemed worthy to play the sport can only play baseball. If we do that, then we become an elitist game. It would game that can only be dreamed about and never one a game that anyone has a chance to be good in.

There is a little bit of Moonlight Graham in all of us. We want to be able to wink at the pitcher as he throws the ball. We come to the game because it brings out the dreamer in each of us. When the player of our favorite team makes the final out in the World Series, we can imagine it is you and I making that final out. When the batter or runner scores the winning run in the bottom of the ninth inning, we imagine it is us that has scored the winning run.

If someone has any chance to play in a major league game, I think they would take it. Jason has a chance to do that this week, if we let him. I don't think I could deny him that chance. I don't think you can, also.

Thank you for giving me this chance to speak.

With that I sat down with Jason and Tim. The floor didn't swallow me up. The roof did not cave in, Jason shook my hand and Tim again just smiled. I guess I got through to a couple of people.

The commissioner signaled Jason to begin his testimony. He walked over to the table where the microphone was situated and shuffled his notes and then he began,

For the first time the crowd quieted. For most of the reporters it was the first time that they would hear a complete story of why he wanted to play baseball. They would judge him as much as those who would pass judgment in the next few hours:

Good afternoon. I know that it is getting late, so I'll try not to make this lengthy. My name is Jason Kowalski and I would like to play baseball.

I had always loved baseball. It has always seemed to me that there are two seasons in which the year is made up. One is baseball season and the other season is the rest of the year.

I was never that great at the sport, but Lord how I loved it! As a kid in my neighborhood we played constantly. In the winter we played any board game of baseball we could find: All star baseball, Strat-o-matic, APBA. Whatever was we played it. We imagined ourselves to be the heroes of the diamond, both past and present. To this day I still play sim baseball: be it Whatifsoorts.com or the Sporting News Stat-o-matic games.

I got better as I grew older, even playing on my high school Team until I had a heart infection that ended my dreams of ever playing baseball again.

About six years ago, my heart condition became worse and I was placed on the list for a heart transplant. I received a heart transplant about two years later. The next two years I spent recovering not only from the transplant, but from a couple of setbacks that sent me in the hospital or rehab center for the next eight straight months.

I eventually recovered and through a lot of therapy got back much of my strength. I went back to my old job at the warehouse in the past year and have had great check ups since getting out of the hospital. For this I thank God for his grace in helping me get well.

Earlier in this summer, I had the audacity to send a request to Oprah for tickets to a Cub game as a treat for a few of my friends and family who had supported me through the long road to recovery. She must have told a friend who works at Wrigley Field and they had told one of the public relations men about me. In part he had hoped we could cop some tickets for a skybox at the ballpark.

Apparently, that publicity person had told someone higher up in the organization and in talking to me found out how much I liked baseball and thought that maybe I could have my dream fulfilled.

When approached, I naturally said yes. It was only was to be one inning and I was never promised to be able to bat or take the field. Possibly it would be as a pinch runner.

I could practice with the team in the week before to get a little taste of big league baseball. Also, I could sit in the dugout during the games that week. It was arranged that I could even travel with the team if they happen to be on the road for the week.

All of this is pretty heady for a 33-year-old guy who had never thought he would ever play baseball again, much less be a part of a professional baseball team. Or for that matter still remain alive.

Now I see that some are saying hold on, maybe this isn't the right thing to do. I can understand some of this. But, in some way I would be disappointed if after all this build up and promise the chance is taken away from me.

I cannot blame the Cubs organization. They have stood by their decision to allow me my chance to play. For that I am grateful. Some that say that only those that we deem acceptable can only play. That disappoints me.

I look at my chance to play as a chance to represent the everyday fan. As Mr. Sweeney said I would represent all of those who ever dreamed of putting on a glove or swinging a bat. I hope you can give me a chance to represent those people.

Thank you for letting me to speak.

The commissioner then spoke. "I and my staff wish to ask you a few questions Mr. Kowalski would you mind if we ask them?'

Jason: Not at all Commissioner. Anything that you need to help you make a decision I will gladly answer.

Commissioner: Jason, do you think that you can play baseball and why do you think that way?

Jason: Yes I do commissioner. Now I won't say I'll play like a superstar. But I think that for one inning I can handle the job. You have to understand that even the best player on any team today will bat no better than .350. Why in the American League we have designated hitters. Some older players that now longer can play on the field keep playing because they still can hit some. In part we have designated hitters because most pitchers are notoriously poor hitters and some fans feel that it brings more offence to the game.

Commissioner: You don't believe that it will hurt you in any way?

Jason: No, who knows it may do me some good, Also just think the kind of example this will have on others who are transplant patients or about to be one!

Commissioner: What about those people who think this kind of stunt will hurt baseball.

Jason: With all due respect Commissioner, you and others may think it's a stunt. I think of it as an inspiration. Other people will see that having dreams and trying to live them is not such a terrible idea after all. Everyone should have something that they and do well and be proud of accomplishing their goal, no matter how lofty or small it is.

Commissioner: Tell me, Mr. Kowalski, in what way will your appearance help baseball?

Jason: I think that this has been alluded to already. I believe it will draw more people to be interested in baseball. Let me give you a couple of examples. In the late 70's George Blanda played football for the Oakland Raiders. He played a number of games for them, leading them to victory. He was in his late forties. His exploits gave many middle age people a chance to be proud and have a wider interest in football. Back in the late sixties there was a field goal kicker with the New Orleans Saints who kicked field goals with only half a foot. Just recently the US women's soccer team won the World Cup. That inspired many girls to take up soccer as a sport. Any time that any one does something unusual in a sport people take an interest.

Commissioner: Thank you Mr. Kowalski, for your candid answers. Is there any thing else that someone would like to bring up?

After that Tim jumped up and stated that He had two more things to bring up in defense of Kowalski. He then presented a number of players that supported Jason being given a chance to play.

Among them were Henry Aaron, Ernie Banks, and Ron Santo. All three remarked that they came from poor families and only through the help of others that they were able to play the game that they loved.

Henry Aaron brought up Jackie Robinson. He told everyone that Jackie endured ridicule, abuse and players who refused to play with him, because of the color of his skin. Yet he played and helped the game improve.

Sammy Sosa commented that everyone should have an opportunity to play if possible. He felt that an exception could be made for someone like Kowalski. That making one small exception was not going to hurt the game, the pay structure or the integrity of the game.

Ernie Banks was the best. In his closing remarks, he allowed that: "If Jason is the baseball fan he claims to be, I'm sure he would want to play TWO today.

He brought down the house.

Then Tim went to the back of the hall and started to talk with a uniformed man. I couldn't make out whom it was but I'm sure it was the person Tim told me to be on the lookout for when he was talking earlier.

Tim came back to the front of the hall and said," I want to present to the commissioner one more piece of evidence. Or should I say several thousand pieces of testimony. I wish to present to you Commissioner the voice of the fan." Turning to a group of US Postal workers, Tim announced, " Gentle men show the Commissioner what you have."

With that several dozen US Postal Service workers began to bring to the front of the hall, bags and bags of letters. There were maybe 30 bags in all.

As they delivered the letters to the commissioners, Tim explained that all of these letters were in support of Kowalski playing baseball for the Cubs.

'In addition." Tim went on to say. "An internet poll was conducted which supported Mr. Kowalski and his desire to play by a margin of 80 to 20 percent."

If Ernie brought down the house, Tim Gavin made it explode. The place was totally out of control. Some shouted that all of this needed to be examined. Others shouted that the evidence should be accepted.

The Commissioner called the meeting to order as best as he could. Then called a recess.

The recess was called because of all the evidence in the meeting that had to be sifted. We certainly gave the Commissioner a lot to sift. I asked Tim how he managed to get all the letters and Internet responses,

"Well," Tim replied. "I got a hold of your editor and convinced him to that it would be a good thing to let the readers respond, with the idea that we would send the responses to Major League Baseball. I also called the editors of the major papers to do the same thing. I also asked the editors to save all the letters that were sent snail mail to the editor to be sent here for the meeting. It was a good publicity stunt for the papers and the editors ate it up."

Tim smiled a little wider. "Besides the editors, the Cub organization got a ton of mail which I used. Your stories evoked a lot of sympathy for Jason, Thank God for that. So, no matter what happens here, Jason will be a celebrity."

Jason shook his head. "All I wanted to do was to play a little baseball. I never expected all of this."

"Better get used to it, kid," I laughed. "I think your life has changed in more ways than you ever imagined.

I turned to Tim. "What's our chances?"

Tim thought a minute then said, "despite it all, maybe 50/50. You have to understand that the Commissioner will have a hard time with his idea of the integrity of the game. It will be hard to let it go and do something totally off in left field."

Just then everyone was called back as the Commissioner had made his decision.

After about 15 minutes the Commissioner entered the room. I couldn't tell one way or the other what way the decision had gone. The room was silent with anticipation. You could almost hear the New York traffic outside in all that silence.

Then the Commissioner spoke:

This case is a most difficult one. I want to congratulate both sides on their presentations. Both had presented arguments that were both well thought out as well as emotional. Both sides should be proud of themselves.

I have always felt strongly about preserving the integrity of the game of baseball (groans from Tim). It is most important to me that gimmicks and wild promotions should not compromise baseball. We can never let those things undercut the purity of the game.

However, this situation is a bit different than that. This is not a wild promotion or a gimmick. It is a gesture to allow one person the ability to play for one inning on a professional baseball team.

Apparently, the fans would enjoy someone like Mr. Kowalski being able to play the game. The amount of letters and e-mails show that they overwhelmingly support this notion.

That being the case, I have decided to approve the request of the Chicago Cubs to have Mr. Kowalski play. Before any one gets excited, I think some restrictions are needed. Kowalski can participate in practice and in pre-game exercises. However, considering the medical history of Mr. Kowalski I have determined that he should not take the field or hit. He can however pinch run. I believe that this is for both his benefit and for the integrity of the game. Do you understand the decision I have made Mr. Kowalski? (Jason nods yes)

"With the decision rendered I herby call these proceedings closed."

That was that. The decision was finally made. Tim seemed slightly disappointed. I told him that it was the best we could do. After all from what I heard this was all that was going to happen anyway.

Jason seemed relieved and happy, shaking our hands he said, "thank, thank you, it's pretty much what I expected. At least I'll have a chance to play. That's all I wanted."

Reporters crowded around, shouting questions.

Q. Are you happy with the decision?

Jason: Yes, it was all that I was expecting.

Q. Are you disappointed that you won't bat or field?

J. No, I'm not that good in fielding or batting. Besides with the Cubs in contention, I don't want to be the one to spoil their chances!

Q. When do you think you will play?

J. I don't know, that will be up to the manager

Q. What if you don't get a chance to play?

J. Well I don't want to hurt the team. Again, I'll do whatever the manager wants.

And on it went, it must have seemed to last for more than an hour. It seemed that we answered the same questions at least ten times in different form.

Finally, noting the time (about 7 pm) and the need for print reporters to file reports, we edged out of the building and to our waiting car.

In the car, we realized how hungry we were. Tim said, "This meal is on me. I know a great place that we can have some peace and quiet and figure what's next."

"That simple," I said. "We have to get back to Chicago and baseball. We lost a lot of time with all this hearing stuff."

So, we got to Tim's favorite New York restaurant and dug into a nice meal. There, I asked Jason if he could tell me about his father, if he wasn't too tired. Jason said that it might be good to talk about him.

Sipping a cup of decaf coffee, Jason began:

I suppose I should say something about my Dad. As you know, he passed away a few years ago, after a stroke. While he couldn't do much in those last couple of months, he was able to communicate with us some.

It was hard on all of our family, especially my mother. But, we got through it as well as we could. You know how it is when anyone of your family may pass away.

I will admit that my dad and I were different from each other as day us to night. I'm for obvious reasons an intellectual type. I have never been the athletic type or one who can work with his hands. I have always thought that perhaps, I have been a bit of a disappointment since I wasn't the same type of person he was.

You know, as I get older, I see more of my Dad in me. There are some of the same mannerisms that I use that my Dad used. While physically, I take after my Mom's side of the family, my thinking and mannerisms are more of my Dad's side of the family.

But, I digress. There are two things around the time of my

Dad's death and my transplant that I often think about.

First, there was the time about a week before his death. All of the family was in his room. He was in pretty poor shape by this time. Worn down by fighting to stay well and all the medical procedures that had been performed on him over the last few months and weeks. You could tell that he was ready to go.

Yet, he hung on. I really think he was trying to hang on more for Mom more than for himself. I'm not sure, but I also think he was hanging on waiting to be reassured that Mom would be taken care of in the event of his death.

Any way, that Sunday while we were all sitting around and talking, I went over to his bedside and just held his hand for a little bit. After all we were there to visit him.

He couldn't talk much by then, His voice barely a whisper. But at that moment, he looked up at me and kind of whispered, "Take care of Mom."

If that was ever an acknowledgement of his passing, I don't know what is. I didn't want to get anyone all excited, especially my mom, so I said to my dad "Don't worry, I'm already bossing Mom around."

My Dad looked up at me and nodded. He understood exactly what I meant that I would take care of Mom, as well as I could.

Now, at that time, this was a pretty hefty promise. I still was on oxygen at the time and still waiting for the transplant. But, my Dad needed to be assured that everything would be taken care of when his time to go arrived.

Five days later, my dad passed away, Two days before his death I was called to Loyola because a possible donor had been found. Fortunately, the donor was found not a good fit and I was sent home.

I guess that God and my dad had already decided that I had to take charge of things for my dad's funeral. Which I did. It was not easy being on oxygen and everything, but I feel I did what was expected of me.

We went through our mourning and all. Yet, let me tell you what happened right about the time of my transplant.

One night I had finally fallen asleep and had a dream. In that dream I ran into my family doctor who led me to a large room. Looking around, I noticed that the room was some kind of morgue. As I was looking around at all the bodies that were in this room, I heard my name being called. I looked around and saw who was calling me. It was my Dad. He was laying on one of these carts and was waving me over to him.

When I got there, he shook my hand and thanked me for what I was doing at home. Then he said, "I know the next few months are going to be tough, but, don't worry, everything will be all right.

I said ok and then I had to leave. After a short while I discovered I had awakened.

I don't remember too many of my dreams. A friend of mine says it's because I tend to meet things head on and probably don't have too many problems roosting around in my subconscious. I don't know if that is true, but it a good an explanation as I have heard yet.

So all of that gave me some hope when I went on to receive my transplant. I felt that my dad and all the relatives that had passed before then would watch out for me and intercede for me to God if things got tough.

CHAPTER 17: ROB AGAIN

When Jason was finished, I could see that he was exhausted. We all were. It was near 10pm and I still had to send out my article to the paper.

Tim said that we had a noon flight out of New York to arrive in Chicago about three hours later. So we climbed into the car and got back to the hotel.

There I sent my report on to the paper:

JASON GETS HIS CHANCE

New York—In a decision by the Commissioner of baseball, Jason Kowalski was given limited permission to play for the Chicago Cubs.

In a rare public hearing in the matter, the Commissioner agreed that Jason could pinch run, but not field or bat, citing concerns for Kowalski's health and for the integrity of the game.

The hearing was raucous at times, both sides presented emotional arguments on why Kowalski should and should not play.

In the end, the case was decided in Kowalski's favor when one of his representatives, Tim Gavin, a Chicago lawyer representing both the Cubs and Kowalski, presented both letters and e-mails that supported Jason's desire to play.

Kowalski declared that he is very happy with the decision and has no problem adhering to the conditions laid down.

Later that evening in an interview with this reporter, Kowalski expressed how a desire to begin the final phase of the process and that he would be thinking of his father as he takes the field in what ever circumstances in the next few days.

Kowalski's father died a couple of years ago and never had the opportunity to see Jason's recovery from his heart problems and would be pleased in his sons efforts if he were alive today.

---

As I finished the story, I realized what a long day it had been. But, I was satisfied that it was all over and we had some how pulled it off. I guess I could call it a day.

CHAPTER 18: DAY FIVE

That morning we gathered at the hotel restaurant for a quick breakfast before going to the airport. It was a quiet meal as all of us were tired after the previous long day.

Also, the Cubs were set to play a 4 game series with the Astros that evening. I knew that Jason would need the time to get ready for the circus that would be following him in the next few days.

I wondered if they would play him immediately that night to get the distraction out of the way or wait until the time was just right to put him in the game. Kowalski seemed unconcerned either way. He was just glad the hearing was over and he could be a part of the game and the team.

Arriving at the airport, we were again mobbed by the press. Again, voicing fatigue and the desire to be left alone we refused all requests for interviews and statements. Tim promised a general statement to be released after we arrived in Chicago. "Right now, what Jason needs is some time to rest and reflect on all the things that have taken place in the last couple of days."

Once the statement was made we got on the jet and soon

were in the air.

Jason and I sat together in the front of the jet while Tim sat in the back to prepare a general statement to be released when we landed in Chicago. "That way we won't be bothered when we arrive and everyone will be happy." Tim said.

But even on the plane we could not get peace and quiet that we wanted. First, there were the fans asking for autographs, which Jason kindly, if tiredly signed, and then there were representatives of magazines and book publishers all asking if Kowalski would be interested on signing a book or magazine deal.

To the magazine representatives he said that he would consider their offers, AFTER he finished playing.

To the book publishers he told them the same thing. When offered ghostwriters to help him with the book, he replied. "If I decide to do the book, I've already made up my mind that Mr. Sweeney will help me write the book. He has helped me so far, and I see no reason to change now."

"You know you'll be rich, kid," I joked.

'If I write the book, I guess so. But, so will you as my ghostwriter."

I waved him off. "Look," I said. "I'll do it if you want, but you don't have to use me. There are others, you know."

"I know," said Jason. "But you have been with me through all of this, so you should get some kind of compensation for your efforts. Besides I can't write as well as you. Anyway, I try to stay loyal to my friends."

With that, we shook hands on the deal. Jason told me if he agrees, Tim would be his agent. I told him that I didn't think that it would be a problem.

As I looked out over the Ohio River valley, Jason asked me if I was a big baseball fan as a kid.

So I told him that I loved baseball ever since I saw a Cubs play a game in 1959. I really got hooked when I saw Don Caldwell pitch a no hitter for the Cubs in 1960. From then on I was hooked on baseball and the Cubs,

I told him about 1969 and the September swoon. To this day I remarked the Cubs didn't so much lose the division title as much as the hated Mets won it.

"After all there were other teams that lost the pennant in a worse way than the Cubs." I told him of the 1964 Philadelphia Phillies. They had a 61/2 game lead with a week to go that year and lost to the St Louis Cardinals. Some called it the biggest swoon of all time in baseball.

There were stories about Mazerouski's home run in 1960 that beat the Yankees in the World Series that year. And of course, Ernie Banks 500$^{th}$ home run.

I remember faking being sick so I could stay at home to watch the game, because I knew that this would be the game that he would do it. I'm sure my parents knew that I was faking, but somehow they went along with it.

I told Jason how I lay there watching the game and how hard it was to fake being ill as Banks circled the bases and Jack Brickhouse was shouting his signature "HEY! HEY!"

We talked about a lot of baseball, Jason and I. We talked about how Gabby Hartnett hit is homer in the gloamin' at Wrigley Field in 1935. How Babe Ruth called his home run at Wrigley in 1932. And about all the greats that had passed through Chicago and the Cubs through out the ages.

Jason asked if the Bambino really called his shot at Wrigley that day, I told him that according to legend he did. Though some thought he was just talking while swinging a few practice swings that happened to look like he was aiming at right field.

"The Cub bench was giving it to Ruth pretty good that day," I related. "You got to remember that this was near the end of Ruth's career. In a couple more years the Yankees released Ruth and he ended his playing time with the Boston Braves. He came back to Boston, the town he left in 1919. He was traded to New York from the Boston Red Sox and started the fabled curse of the Bambino that lasted until the Red Sox won the World Series recently."

I talked again about Banks hitting his 500$^{th}$ homerun. I told him that it was one of the most important sport events that ever took place in Chicago. I was glad I was able to see it on T.V., if I couldn't see it live.

Tim came over to show us his statement that will be given to the press when we arrived in Chicago. I asked him if he was a baseball fan. He answered "not really. I'm more of a Notre Dame football fan." Seems that Tim had graduated from Notre Dame and while not much for sports he always rooted for the Fighting Irish,

"How did you pick up this gig?" Jason asked. "Well" said Tim." The Cubs are one of my firm's clients. And when I heard about Jason and his problem with major league baseball, I asked that I be assigned to the case. I haven't been disappointed yet."

With that he went back to his seat and Jason and I continued our conversation.

Jason then asked me "I know that it's none of my business. But what happened that made you leave Chicago and end up in Mesa, Arizona?"

I thought about it a few minutes and decided to tell Jason what had happened. I had tried to forget about all of those days and just get on with my life. But somehow, somewhere I had to come to terms with my past if I ever wanted to live in the future.

Getting another cup of coffee from the flight attendant, I began to tell my story…

Back around seven years ago, I was a hotshot sports reporter for a large paper in Chicago. Besides my regular beat covering the Cubs and Bears, I had a regular weekly sports column that was syndicated across the nation.

In the column I looked at the sports scene on a national level and exposed some of the less savory aspects of sports.

It was about that time I received reports that certain players in minor league baseball were using steroids in violation of the policy of baseball. I reported the findings after checking and rechecking my sources. The evidence all seemed plausible and true, so I published the facts as they were related to me and it caused quite a stir.

I was riding high on the basis of that expose. I did not name any one publicly, but gave the names over to Major League Baseball and hoped to see them take care of their problem. At that time I had more faith in the sport taking care of their problem than I do now.

I kept up the pressure calling for investigations and for baseball to clean up their mess. Yet, I felt nothing was being done.

One day, A few weeks after the initial story broke. Jim Hudson, the sport editor for the paper called me into his office. In his office were some other people, whom I recognized as the investigating team of major league baseball.

As I might have said before Jim and I did not see eye to eye on a lot of things. I always thought of him as a yes man to the publisher and I'm certain he saw me as a threat.

Younger than I, Jim had risen quickly in the world of journalism. A competent writer, I guess his strength was mainly being well organized and able to work well under great pressure.

I guess he feared that if I wanted, I could take over his position, due to my popularity as a columnist for the paper. What he didn't realize is that I didn't really want his position. I was happier with writing and reporting, rather than doing administrative tasks.

If he had taken the time to talk to his reporters, instead of talking about them he would have made a lot more friends and would have been a more effective editor.

Jim sat down at his desk, and asked me, "Rob, how well do you trust your sources on that steroid story?"

"Well, pretty good," I replied, "Why?"

"These people are from Major League baseball and have been doing an extensive investigation and have found out that the players you accused of taking steroids are innocent and that the person or persons that gave you the information may have faked the documents that they supplied to you." Jim just shook his head.

I was stunned. I trusted my sources implicitly. I had worked hard to get the correct information and thought I had done a thorough job. Now I find that my information was tainted.

"Look, I know that my sources were telling me the truth. I

would never use tainted information, never!" I was devastated and confused at that point.

One of the investigators spoke up. "We have the original physical reports. They are different than the one you gave to Major League Baseball." He showed me the original physicals and compared them to the one I had given to Major League Baseball and used as the basis my stories.

I went back to my original notes and documents and in looking closely at them and comparing them to the original documents, I could see that something had been changed.

Jim spoke up again. "The players that you accused privately are angry, Rob, they're after your hide. They figure that you made the charge, you should be made to pay."

Jim sighed, Look, unless we can get to the bottom of who was wrong, I'll have to do something drastic.

I swallowed and thought and they'll fire me for sure, if I can't come up with some hard evidence. I told them that if they gave me some time I'd check with my main source and see what happened. The investigators said that it sounded fair, but with emotions running high, they could only give me about 24 hours.

With that, I immediately went back to my office and got on the phone and called my source. "Where did you get your information!" I screamed. I must have sounded like a lunatic to anyone within earshot of me. The investigators from major league baseball are after me for an explanation and I'm sure the paper will be sued if the story hurts any player and their chances of getting a baseball job! I was pretty much beside myself.

Hold on; Hold on, my source shot back. "My information is correct; maybe it's the investigators that are snowing you."

I thought about that, it could be true, but at that moment it was their word against my source, himself a former baseball player that didn't make it to the big leagues.

I was trapped. I couldn't expose my source, and he couldn't give me any more proof than he already had. Yet, what the investigators had looked pretty authentic to me. Who was lying? I didn't know. But the end result would be the loss of my job and a possible lawsuit. Either way, I was in for the worst time of my professional career.

I called it a day at work. Went out downed a few drinks and when I finally got home late that night, called my lawyer, Ben Attlee.

Ben was an old guard New Englander, tall and white haired. He is as somber as he was plain spoken. He is as straightforward as a New England snowstorm. I valued his judgment as much as I valued anybody. He told me straight out when I told him what had happened, that I had been set up. It doesn't matter by whom but I was going to have to play some kind of price.

He then told me if the worst that can happen is the loss of the job, and then consider myself lucky. "You cold be sued for libel, but the paper will probably cut a deal with baseball so their liability is protected. I'm sure that the loss of your job will be the price to avoid a lawsuit on libel charges. Only fight if they cut you off without a lifeline."

The next day, all of us met in my editor's office and a deal was cut. Attending the meeting was myself and Ben, the investigators and lawyers from major league baseball, and the newspaper lawyers and Jim.

My editor spoke first. "Rob, the story has put the paper in an untenable situation. We could fight the charges leveled against you, but the evidence against you is strong and there is some doubt that we can prevail. Also, it would put you in a lot of hot water, which I'm sure can be avoided. We want to keep your name out of things, but we can't do with out help from you."

At that point I knew the fix was in and I was screwed. Jim continued. "What we want from you is for you to resign your post and baseball will drop the investigation. No one will be charged and no lawsuits will be filed. I'm only sorry that you will be the one who will have to pay a price here. But it's the only way the situation can be resolved."

I wondered how late the lawyers stayed up to work out that deal. I looked at Ben and he shrugged "it's to you. Remember what we talked we talked about last night. You know my recommendation."

So, I agreed. With in the hour I packed my box with my awards and other personal effects said good-by to a few old friends and walked out the door of the office never to look back until I came back a few days ago.

The next five years were spent in a funk. Without my job at the paper I was lost. I drank a little, but I never was much of a drunk so that never lasted. I was depressed for a while. I was so depressed that after a couple of years my wife left me.

I couldn't find a job in the Immediate Chicago area, so I tried Indiana. But, after being out for a couple of years, people do forget you. I tried the newspapers in Hammond, Gary, South Bend and Michigan City. All of them either said that they didn't have an opening, or weren't interested. I guess the news of my dismissal was still too fresh in their minds.

That didn't help me much so I did a little traveling and tried to pick up some writing jobs or for that matter any other jobs that I could find.

Eventually, I ended up in Embudo, New Mexico. There an old friend, Laura, found me a job at a restaurant, waiting on tables. I did manage to sell a couple of freelance articles, but, sports' reporting was still in my blood and I really wanted to get back to working in that capacity.

I had known Laura when she worked as a nutritionist at the hospital where I once worked while in college. Then, she was a free spirit back then and still is. She worked with an Indian reservation helping the Indians there get the type nutritional help that they needed and worked out of a free clinic.

Doing the job for the last 25 years had not dulled her. She still was up beat and enthusiastic, despite a painful injury to her legs, forcing her to use crutches.

Laura was the one person who encouraged me and helped me the most when I needed it.

She was also the one who told me it was time to move on and find another reporting job. She wanted me to get the hell off my butt and get back to living, instead of feeling sorry for my self.

I wrote some free lance sports articles and used them as part of my resume. One resume I sent to the paper in Mesa, Arizona. It was there that I met Max, my present editor.

I was bold about it this time around. I told him that I'm good, have the experience and no matter what you heard I always try to do an accurate job in reporting the story.

Max looked at me and countered, "I know all about what happened in Chicago. Let me tell you something I don't care what happened there. I only care about what you do here. Mesa might be just the place to get you settled. It's a laid back town where the people only care about what you can do now, not what you did in the past. I think this would be just the place for you to get back on your feet again. Why would I know? Because I have been through some of the same things you have been through. Don't ask me about that, because I won't tell you. And, don't tell me about all of your troubles. I don't want to know. Just do your job and we'll get along fine."

The money wasn't much and the perks were not the best. I took the job.

Max and I have a good working relationship. We're not drinking buddies and we don't socialize a whole lot, but he supports what I write and he saw a chance for me in this assignment. As a boss he would rank as one of the best I have ever had.

Tim had come over to us as I had finished my tale and said, "From what I heard, you sure have had some rough times. I hope this story brings you whatever you're looking for."

I reflected a minute and said that I'll probably figure out what all of this means about a couple of months from now. "I tend to be a slow thinker, that's why I write, and become a sportscaster not a lawyer."

The pilot announced that we would be landing soon, so we got ready for Chicago. As I looked down at the Windy City, I found a new awareness about myself. I came to an awareness that it would always be home to me, but never be home again. I found that I rather stay in Arizona and live the quieter life. Enjoy what I have now because I may never have it again.

As we got off the plane and made our way through the terminal, we were met by a crush of reporters and cameramen. All eye were upon us will Tim passed out the prepared statement.

On the statement Tim said that Jason appreciated the interest and welcome back he has received, but now he needs time to get ready to play baseball and join the Cubs in practice as they had a night game to play. Comment will be made after he finally plays.

We rushed to the waiting car and flew down the Dan Ryan to Wrigley to meet the team for the second time.

The traffic was bad as we came closer to Wrigley Field. The Cubs were still in the wild card hunt and the usual 39,000 fans would be at the park again.

Entering the locker room Jason was greeted more like a savior than a nuisance. Almost all the players greeted him warmly, even the players called up from the minors, all but one.

The Cubs had called up a catcher from their Triple A Iowa team. Jerry Morris was a short but stocky kind of guy. About 30 years old, he had slowly moved up through the Cubs' farm system and had a good year at the bat for Iowa this past year.

He was kind enough to Kowalski bit still seemed a little wary. There was something about him that I couldn't put my finger on. Something that I thought I should know but the connection eluded me at that moment.


But now the attention was squarely on Jason. Reporters buzzed around and Jason gave them general answers. He was getting to be a pro at managing the press. "I guess you won't be needed as a press agent," I said to Tim.

"It doesn't matter," he replied. "But if you don't mind, I think I'll stick around and see how the story ends."

At that Tim said he has a seat with his family to watch the game and left for a while. He invited me to come with him and I said that I would after checking in with the office.

On the way out I ran into the Cubs manager and asked him if Jason will get his chance to play tonight. He said that it might be possible, but he would rather wait a couple more days and maybe play him over the weekend. " I want to give him a couple of days to decompress after the meeting with the Commissioner and all the fuss in New York."

I agreed. Jason was tired after the last few days and he needed to get better situated. Tonight would be too early.

Jason took batting practice and actually did not do bad. He even got a couple of grounders, which surprised me. Maybe he could have batted, I thought to myself. The Commissioner is all wet, I thought.

The game itself was close all the way to the end. The Cubs won on a bases loaded walk in the bottom of the ninth. After the game, reporters gathered around Jason for his reaction to the contest and not yet playing.

"I'm glad we won," he laughed. "If I can help the team win games by sitting on the bench, then, I'm all for it." He winked at the reporters and to the manager and I standing off on the side. His comment brought down the house and everyone left with a story that they could file.

Tim and I took Kowalski home. We were both tired and giddy after 2 days of pressure and long flights. Jason was greeted as a hero from the gathered neighbors at his home. He thanked everyone for coming by and for their support, but if they didn't mind, he needed rest.

As Jason walked me over to my car I told him. "You know we still haven't talked about the transplant or the long recovery."

He shook my hand and said, "I know, I know. How about we take a walk by the lake in the morning and we can over that."

I agreed and he patted me on the back. When I got to the hotel, I filed another story and settled in for a nice long sleep. Then I dreamed about spring training in Mesa where I got the call to play full time with the Cubs

.

CHAPTER 19: DAY SIX-ROB

I got up early that next morning and decided to amuse myself with breakfast in the hotel room. As I was finishing my coffee and thinking about getting ready and meeting Jason for another interview, the telephone rang. It wasn't my editor, but rather my soon to be ex-wife, Brenda.

"Well, hello," she said. "Thought you could get away from Chicago without hearing from me?"

I admit I hadn't thought it was the best time to think about a visit, since we were in the middle of a divorce. But we had tried to remain friends, despite the problems over the last couple of years.

"No, I've been distracted by all the work on my assignment and going back and forth to New York and here." It was true, although I could have called.

"Yeah, I saw your articles. They're in all the papers. It must feel nice to be on top again." I thought I heard a little bit of pride in her voice, something I hadn't heard from her for a long time.

She couldn't see me shrug over the phone so I just said thanks and asked her from where she was calling.

"From work." She worked as the head nurse in ICU at the University Medical Center of Chicago.

"I wonder if you have time to meet me for lunch?" Now that

was a surprise.

I told her that I had an interview and a game tonight and tomorrow during the day. Perhaps we can have dinner tomorrow evening?

She answered that she could make it, although she might be on call. "It's the nature of the job you know."

I could relate to that since our jobs were part of the reason we were apart, besides me acting like a fool after being fired.

I agreed and set up a time to meet. Then hung up the phone. I lay on my bed and decided to indulge myself on what had happened in our marriage and whose fault it was. Most of the time I took the blame.

Brenda and I met while in college. I was studying journalism and she was studying to be a nurse. We both had a class in creative writing, I needed it for my major and she needed it to fill out her English requirements.

When she needed help on one of her stories, she asked me for advice. Now Brenda was just average in looks, but she had an upbeat personality. So, despite myself, I came to enjoy her company. Soon we were dating and were together often when we weren't studying like mad.

Actually, I asked her out in a most unusual way.

It seemed that one day I was reading some announcements in the school newspaper and came across an announcement that 'victims' were needed for a mock emergency drill that would be attended by a lot of the student nurses as a way to give them some experience in the real world. Dealing with a emergency situation.

I thought that it would be a kick to be involved in the project and signed on.

I was given the assignment to play a difficult patient that had a head wound. It sounded like fun and I practiced like mad to make sure I got the right tone to pull it off.

When I got to do my part I laid it on thick, yelling and screaming and moaning and groaning. I was really into it.

Lo and behold Brenda was to be the nurse in this little drama. I did my best to make it difficult for her. When she tried to bandage me, I even fought her.

"Hold still, you idiot!" She was not amused.

I told her that her bedside manner needed a bit of work. "You can't say that to a hurt and confused patient. What type of nurse do you think you are?"

"A nurse with a smart alack, loud mouth patient," She replied. "Some one who doesn't take orders too well"

"Look," I told her. "I'm doing what my card says, you want this to be as realistic as possible, don't you?"

"Yes, but..." She obviously was losing it. I thought I should make it a little easier on the both of us.

I made a deal with her. "I'll play the nice sedated patient and help you out but you got to do me one favor."

"What's that?" She said.

Just go out with me."

We went out a few days later. She was funny and bright, as I thought she would be. I was funny and bright, or at least that's what she told me. We spent the next couple of years together as a college couple learning all we can about each other before deciding to get married.

With the future awaiting us, we figured that out work would complement each other and we would never be bored of frustrated. We would find out soon enough how wrong that could be.

After college I got a job on a small suburban paper and she found a nursing position in the nearby town. We saw each other as often as possible and figured that if we are going to see each other this much, we might as well get married.

The first years were happy one, although, we found that we couldn't have children. That didn't bother us much; we were more interested in our careers more than anything else.

Soon I was on the big Chicago paper and Brenda found her dream job as a nurse in ICU at the University Medical Center. As always, with our careers taking off, we had little time to notice that we had changed.

When the scandal hit and I lost my job everything changed. It was the realization that having our careers had become the main focus in our marriage. I guess we hadn't grown as much as we had thought in the intervening years.

To Brenda's credit, she did try to take everything in stride, She said not to worry, take my time in trying to figure out what I wanted to do next, we can live on her salary and my severance pay while I got it together.

I wasn't so blessed. I was depressed started drinking and realized that drinking wasn't the answer either.

I stopped drinking, but I was still depressed. So much so I didn't want to get out of the house. Brenda urged me to look elsewhere in the area for a position and I figured that I had nothing to lose.

So I went all over, but nothing happened.

As I moved further out in search of a writing position, Brenda became more and more opposed to moving anywhere out of the area. She had taken a position as the head nurse in the ICU and was enjoying the experience. I couldn't blame her. The money was great and the status unassailable. She was happy and I was as dark minded as I could be.

I needed to get back to work fulltime. I had written a couple of freelance articles that had sold, but the assignments were not near enough to ease my pain.

That's when I decided that I had to look further outside the Chicago area if I was ever to find a decent job.

When I told Brenda this, she was furious. "How could you do that!" She screamed. "You know how important my career is to me. We're doing fine without you working full time. Just keep writing the freelance material and the rest will follow."

The rest of the marriage suffered as we dealt with the problems that I had. I suppose I could have been happy with just writing freelance articles and eventually something would have come along. But In part I needed to do more. Having a full time job validated me and made me feel that what had happened was not my fault. That's how I looked at it any way.

Finally, I got a job writing for a paper in Springfield, Illinois. Brenda was livid that I dared take the job. I explained again how important it was for me to work. I was not the type to sit around doing nothing. She still did not want to give up her position in Chicago. We were at an impasse.

At that point we decided to live separately. We agreed that we would try things out long distance. I had my doubts, but I was willing to try. In spite of everything we still loved each other. If one if us wouldn't be so stubborn. Of course each of us thought the other was the stubborn one.

Soon I had an offer to work in St. Louis, Missouri. I thought that for sure I could convince Brenda to come down and work there. She refused, saying that the move wasn't right for her and that the experience of working in one of the top hospitals in the nation was all the challenge she needed.

At that point, I gave up. I decided that if that's what she wanted, than, that's what she'll get.

It didn't help me much, however. I became more depressed than earlier. I couldn't concentrate in my job and the paper just let me go.

I continued to wander around. Even taking odd jobs here and there to make ends meet, No matter what however, I refused to go back to Brenda with my tail between my legs. I was stubborn to a fault. I would go down stubborn if it meant keeping my pride.

I eventually up in Embudo, New Mexico, where Laura helped me out. She took me in and then found me a job at the restaurant.

When the sport-reporting job opened up in Mesa, she said to me, "You know you want it," Laura said. Besides you're lousy at waiting on tables. You have a terrible attitude, and only writing is going to mellow you out. Either go back home to your wife or go after the job."

I decided that she was right. I went to the interview and got the job.

A couple of months later Brenda informed me that she wanted a divorce. I knew than it was over. I didn't feel mad, glad or anything. Except for a few telephone conversations we had little contact with each other. I guess out of sight, out of mind trumps absence makes the heart grow founder. But, I will admit I think of Brenda almost every day.

I shook myself out of my reverie. Time to go see and pick up Jason and hear more of his story.

I arrived at Jason's house about 11:45 am. He was already waiting for me when I pulled up. He climbed in the car and said. "Let's go to the lakefront in Whiting, Indiana. It's quiet and has a pier we can walk out on. Then I can tell you a little more about my time before the transplant."

Whiting is a small, land locked town with Lake Michigan on it's north side You might think of it as the town that time forgot until you see that it is the host to one of the largest oil refineries in the world.

Despite all of that it's a quaint town. Named for 'pop' Whiting who had ditched a train to save some residents on a train track, Of course he was driving too fast. So the incident either made him the bravest person ever to ditch a train or the biggest fool to be driving a train so fast.

It's also home of the pierogi festival. Each August people in the town dress up as pierogi's. This is a favorite food of the polish decedents of the town. Each year they celebrate the food with silly but all in good fun parties, polkas and parades.

The lakefront is part of a park, which holds a fourth of July celebration each year.

The pier is made of iron that juts out to the water. There you can glimpse the skyline of Chicago, if your view isn't obscured by the smoke of the steel mills that make up the view on the other side of the pier.

At this time of the year the lakefront and the park is quiet as the celebrations of the summer are long over. It becomes a perfect place to think, write, play guitar, make out or just have a long intimate talk with your friend.

Perhaps if I knew of this place years ago, Brenda and I would still be together. We could have walked out on the pier and talked thing out in a calm manner.

As it was it became a perfect place for Jason to tell me more of his story.

CHAPTER 20: JASON CONTIUES HIS STORY

The 13 months that I waited for the transplant were the longest and hardest of my life. That is until I was recovering from the transplant. I was hooked up to a concentrator, which took oxygen out of the air and sent it to me through a nasal cannula.

It was like having a tail. I had to drag the 50-foot tubing all through the house. It was continually on and kind of restricted where I could go in the house. I continued to try to keep walking, as I wanted to be in the best shape possible when I eventually received my transplant.

I would walk through the house, about 50 feet each way. Walking as much as I could, I would try to do about 50 laps. It was a rough walk, some days I was extremely tired but at least I was walking.

That meant rolling up and unrolling the tubing as I walked. It was a hassle that I never enjoyed. But, I was determined to keep walking and moving as much as I could.

I used a portable system when I went any where outside the house. I felt like I was getting ready to go out with a weapon, making sure I had enough ammunition to make it through the jungle outside.

Only once I was foolish enough to not bring enough ammo with me. I had gone out with a friend whom was kind enough to take me to Loyola for a check up while waiting for the transplant.

Now I know how Lee felt at Appomattox, running out of ammo, food and men. Here I was running out of air. I was on my last tank and I thought I had enough for the trip home. I looked at the oxygen level on the tank and saw that it was almost out. Apparently, I had taken a tank that was partly used and didn't realize it.

I was embarrassed. I told my friend that I had goofed and we had better hurry back home.

My friend fairly flew home. But it was too late. The oxygen ran out about 10 miles from home. I did make it breathing slowly and deeply, but toward the end it was tough. When I got to the house I told my mom to turn on the concentrator and took a few deep breaths of oxygen. What a relief it was!

It was the last time I ever did that. From now on I made sure that the tanks were full and that I had plenty of them when I went out.

 So you can that getting ready to go anywhere was a hassle and a half. We had to make sure that I had enough tanks of oxygen and have them near by. It sort of was like having enough ammunition when army troops were going on a mission. It was such a headache that I went out less and less.

For the most part I was doing all right. I did worry about when I might be called by around November. I wanted Social Security to cover everything rather than my insurance from work. If Social Security covered the transplant, my prescription bills would be covered. But that was not to happen.

About the time I was about to ask to be put on hold for a couple of months. The hospital called me to have the transplant. Like any movie or book, for dramatic affect they called me about 1:30 am on December 10<sup>th</sup>. They sent someone to get me and I prepared to get what I needed, Like I said before what God wants, God gets. That's how I saw it and I had to follow my talisman all the way through.

But I see it's time to get ready for the game tonight. I'd better go home and get my jacket. It looks like a cool evening for a game. I wonder if tonight's the night.

CHAPTER 21: ROB SPEAKS AGAIN

I had dinner at Kowalski's place with his mom and a couple of other friends. Then drove out to Wrigley for the game.

It was a cooler evening than the night before, but with Jason as a drawing card and a wild card berth still up for grabs, the usual packed hose was expected.

To gauge the crowd reaction in case Kowalski played, I sat in the stands, on the third base side of home, just above the Cubs dugout. I arranged for Tim and his family to join me.

About a half an hour before the start of the game, Tim, his wife and his two daughters joined me. I asked Tim how the day has been for him.

"I'm not getting much work done," shaking his head in frustration and wonderment. "As soon as I get involved in a problem at work or a case, someone from the press calls me up to talk about Jason and his desire to play with the Cubs, I suppose I'll get some work done after all of this us over. I'd work at home but Kathy, my wife says that it's the same thing at home. I'll try to work there, anyway. Maybe the family can run interference and say I'm out with a client. Then I won't be bothered as much."

While we were talking, people get coming and interrupting us. They either wanted a comment or offered encouragement to Jason. Some even wanted my autograph! I indeed obliged them, though I would think that a baseball player would get a lot more on the market than a half washed up journalist.

Soon the game began. From the beginning you can see that it was going to be a close one. With the game in the sixth inning and tied in a pitchers duel at 1 to 1, a strange thing began to happen.

I suppose it was all the tension that had built up over the last few days. Or maybe it was the frustration of the Cubs fans over the long year of waiting and figuring that anyone new might turn the tide around, but the crowd started to call out for Jason to be inserted in the lineup.

It started as a small groan. With in minutes it grew a shout that finally drew into a crescendo as the game moved into the eighth inning.

Between shout of "Kowalski, Kowalski!' or "Jason, Jason!" there were the complaints.

"C'mon, let the kid play!" or "The manager is chicken!" and worse was being said. When the manager came out to take out the starter at the top of the ninth, the crowd really let him have it.

I guess no one had read the paper or refused to believe the announcement the night before that Jason would not get his chance to play until the day games over the weekend.

The Cubs lost the game 3 to 2 in the ninth on an Astro home run, Afterward the press gathered round the Cub manager and asked, no, I would say demanded to know why Kowalski did not play.

The manager answered calmly, "The game was close. We're in a play off race and I thought that I made it clear that Kowalski would not get a chance to play until the weekend afternoon games,'

All of that was true. The press asked Jason how he felt and again he said that he understood. "I don't want to be the reason why the Cubs lost the wild card race, after all I don't want to be Steve Bartman!"

Again the press roared with laughter.

That night we went home, tired but happy that another day was over. I still had one more thing to do, write my story for the paper. When a got to the hotel, I opened my laptop and started to write.

---------------------------------------------------------------------------------

THE TIME IS NOW

Chicago---- After the game tonight the Cubs have two games left. Two games where they will have to find a way to keep a promise to Jason Kowalski.

They need to let him take the diamond for that one time in order to show both Kowalski and the world that when they make a promise to someone they will do everything to keep it.

For the last two days, the Cub organization has kept Jason under wraps. It was done In part to give Jason a chance to become acclimated to the world of professional baseball and to find a good time to let him fulfill his dream.

It's understandable that the Cubs may be reluctant to play Kowalski. They are battling for a play off spot. It is a spot that did not seem possible when they offered the chance to let him play. Now, however it is time to make the promise a reality. It is time for Cub management to sink or swim, to fish or cut bait.

They have put themselves in a spot. They are in a pennant race that they want to win. But they made a promise to a fan.

Decency demands that they fulfill that promise. The public demands it. The fan in the stands demands it. The integrity of the game demands it.

With the big money that is flashed around in baseball and all the Ill will that has followed the game in recent years. It would be good to see baseball so something small for Jason and for the fans.

Let's hope that baseball does the right thing and allows Jason his chance to play.

-----------------------------------------------------------------------------

With that I finished for the night and sent my story for the paper. Then after finishing my cup of coffee, I decided to call it a night and go to bed.

The next day early in the morning, I heard a knock at my door. Groggily, I got up and answered it. To my surprise it was Jason. "Seems that I couldn't sleep," he announced. "I know that in the next two days this will be all over and I haven't told you much about the transplant or the recovery. Would you want to go out for breakfast and we can talk about it? It's my treat."

It seemed like a good idea. I was due to meet my soon to be ex-wife that evening and I wouldn't have a lot of time after tomorrow for talking. So I got washed up and dressed and had a nice breakfast courtesy of my buddy, Jason.

CHAPTER 22: JASON TELLS MORE

First thing you have to know is that I was of mixed emotions about the whole deal. I know that if everything turned out right, I'll have a great recovery. But, there's always a chance things will be rough. As it was I had it rough. The transplant was a rousing success. It was the recovery that was hell.

As I said before they called me in the middle of the night.

Isn't that always the case? Just like in a book or a movie. Well they did. I had it arranged that they would have someone pick me up.

I showered and got ready. I made my bed and picked up my bag that I had ready for the trip to the hospital. The bag was sitting there like I was pregnant and was waiting for the baby to arrive at any moment and planned to go to the hospital. I e-mailed my sister telling her that I'm off to transplant land and that I'll see her on the flip side. Then took one last look around my rooms and went downstairs to wait.

The driver came in about 45 minutes and we took about a 45-minute trip to Loyola. The driver usually picked up doctors in an emergency, but occasionally picked up transplant patients, also.

My mom went with me and it was a pretty quiet ride. I suppose both of us were lost in our own thoughts as I was heading into surgery. I know I was.

After going through the admitting process, the sent a wheel chair along and got me to pre- op and the long wait began. It's usually that way in these types of surgery. Sort of like the Army, hurry up and wait.

There were times even then, when I thought that all of this was unnecessary. That is until I remembered having to use oxygen and not being able to work, play and enjoy things as I did before I became ill. That made me more anxious to get the transplant going.

After about 5 hours of waiting, I was prepared for the transplant. One thing that is given to you is the anti rejection medication. That's when you really know that it won't be long and there's no turning back.

How did I feel at that time? Both excited and also scared. For anybody this is a brave new world. If all goes well, another person's body parts are going to make you well. That's quite a gift. That's also quite a miracle. It is something that boggles the mind both physically and spiritually. If you don't realize that when it happens to you, perhaps you are dead, at least on spirit.

I often imagined what it would be like after the transplant. One time I wrote about it. I called the small piece 'The Operation'

----------------------------------------------------------------------------

        The doctors came in and ripped out my heart and such and put in a new one. I became very intelligent, like Einstein and Freud. I no longer wanted to read my Superman comic books or watch The Beverly Hillbillies. I became almost boring.

----------------------------------------------------------------------------

That's it just fifty words. That's what I imagined my transplant to be. Of course it wasn't. It is much more. At the time it was the best way I could grapple with the reality of what was going to take place. I would learn later how much more it was.

Finally, they came for me. I told my mom I would see her later and was wheeled into the surgery area. There I was prepped and a short time later was given a shot and out I went...

The transplant took about 81/2 hours. I guess I woke up about a day and a half later. To this day, I'm not sure. One thing about a traumatic surgery such as a transplant, your sense of time gets lost. It took me about a week to figure out what day and time it was. Days and night were mixed; the days of the week are confused.

Let me give you an example. One of the male nurses asked if I wanted to watch the Bears game on TV. I said sure I thought it was a Saturday game and became confused when they were showing so many games on TV. I didn't realize it was really Sunday. That meant I lost more than one day when I was out after the transplant.

This made for long days and nights since my sleeping patterns were put out of whack. I never knew if it was day or night. So, it was hard to get acclimated once again. I was living in a time warp and everything was either moving very fast or very slow. Although I was aware of people going in and out of the room, sometimes it all seemed like a dream, rather than reality.

Slowly, I was getting my strength back. By around the third day, they had me out of bed and sitting in a chair. I was eating some and I was feeling better. I did have some fluid in my lungs at times but the doctors thought it would clear up in time. Breathing was getting easier also. Each small step was a big thing for me. I meant one less day in the hospital and a chance to get home soon.

One thing I noticed that I did lose is my voice. When they cut your organs out, a lot of the nerve endings are lost, especially the nerves that connect to your voice box. It sometimes comes back, but mine never really did, although I think it has improved some.

The doctors gave me the ok to start walking around and I did. When the nurses checked how my blood oxygen was, they found it getting better. Although I had to take it slowly, just being able to walk around made me feel that I was going to get better and be out and about soon.

The last four or five days I spent in a regular hospital room. Which was great. I figured I would be home soon. I also was walking the halls. Not far, mind you, but enough to feel encouraged and eager to get home.

I still felt tired at times and I still had some fluid in the lungs. But, I was reassured that it would soon disappear and I would be feeing much more better than I was.

On December 23, they sprung me. Just in time for Christmas and enjoying being at home. It was both happy and sad in a way. It was the first Christmas my dad wasn't around to celebrate with us. I have always thought that my dad would have got a kick at seeing me well again. Although I rather think he has seen me well. Only it is in a better place for him.

Still there were times I didn't feel all that great. But, I was told that there were going to be days that you would feel like an old dirty dishrag, so I just chalked it up to days like that rather than any thing else.

When I went for my first clinic visit after the transplant they were concerned that I still had some fluid in my lungs and decided to do another tap of my lungs to get some of it out.

After the tap, which lasted about an hour, they were satisfied that they got the fluid out and sent me home. I did feel better. I continued to try walking around at home, like I did before and tried to eat a little. Yet, It was hard to eat, mostly because it was so hard to swallow. I always figured it was because of the surgery and all the suctioning that they had to do. I don't know if there was any other explanation.

There were times I was feeling better, but they were getting less and less frequent. I was wondering how long the bad days were going to last. Will it be a week, a month or longer? I figured I would ask some hard questions when I went back to clinic in a few days.

Unfortunately, I never got there. By January 7th I was so bad I could barely hold my head up. After talking to the doctors at Loyola I was rushed to the local hospital with postoperative pneumonia.

I almost did not make it there. A long time was spent in getting me stable. Most of the time I was unconscious. The rest of the time was a blur. I hardly remember the ambulance ride, except for the sirens. I remember nothing of the emergency room.

Eventually, I was stable enough to be sent to Loyola. I was sent there by helicopter. I remember being put in the helicopter and thinking to myself, "good, I can watch how this is done and watch the scenery. No such chance. Soon I was out again and didn't wake up until I was safely at Loyola. It might have been a few days later.

When I did wake up, I discovered I was on a respirator. That machine was going to be my good buddy in the next 6 to 7 months. I also didn't fully realize where I was.

I suppose I had heard someone mention something about Cleveland along the way, so I thought I was at the Cleveland Heart Institute. Of course, I wondered how my family was going to visit me all the way out there. It was about a day or two later that I realized I was at Loyola.

Now here is something funny. I didn't have my glasses on when I was laying there. There was this nurse, who was pretty old taking care of me. Since I didn't have my glasses on I guess I was seeing double. So, at first, I thought that there were TWO little old nurses taking care of me!

It took a while but at least I figured out the day of the week, if not the date. I was uncomfortable, miserable and tired. I didn't want to do anything. I couldn't even move much between all the tubes and the respirator. The best time I spent was sleeping as much as I could, considering all the things that were going on.

You never know how painful it is to have a tube down your throat. It kind of makes your mouth sore. It is the most uncomfortable feeling one could have.

Slowly, I got stronger and was able to even sit up a little. Slowly the fluid in my lungs was getting less and less. Within a few days they took me off the respirator and I was just using oxygen.

With all the improvements, I was feeing more and positive about the eventual outcome. It soon became apparent that I didn't even need the oxygen. I thought that in a few days I could be home.

On January 17th, I had another set back. Seems that my aortic artery developed a leak. When the respiratory therapist came to give me a breathing treatment, I was coughing up blood. I was rushed back to surgery.

I was told that I was going back to fix a small problem, when actually it was a major surgery. Lasted 11 and 1/2 hours. Longer than the original transplant surgery. This was mainly because they couldn't find where the leak was coming from. The eventually found it.  It was underneath my heart. That's the reason the whole surgery took so long.

When I woke up, I was back where I started. I was on my back, with the respirator tube in my throat and a feeding tube through my nose.

On top of all of that, I was so weak I couldn't even move my legs. I guess 18 hours of major surgery in three weeks will do that to you.

If there ever was a time that I ever felt frustrated, it was then. I kept thinking were all the assurances from God and my dad (the dream, you know). I kept thinking that maybe it was all just my imagination. Maybe all this talk of God answering your prayers was just a bunch of hot air. To say I was mad was an understatement. The doctors kept thinking I was depressed. I wasn't, I was angry. My anger did me well in the end when it was time get up and start living.

The doctors wanted to give me an anti-depressive. I refused after taking one that only heightened my dreams to such a level that it bothered me. Finally I told them that I would not take any more anti-depression drugs. "Look, Doc'" I told him. "I'm not depressed, I'm mad. Let me stay mad. It's probably the best way I can deal with all of this. Besides if I learn how to harbor my anger. It will be the best way I could get better and out of here."

I knew the next few months were going to be hard. I didn't realize that it would be eight months before I would get home.

CHAPTER 23: ROB AGAIN

I could have listened to Jason the rest of the day. But looking at my watch, I noticed that it was near time to get to Wrigley Field and the game.

Jason and I got in my Focus and took off. We arrived at Wrigley in time for Jason to get ready for practice. I stopped the manager and asked "Is it today?" He answered, "If everything goes right, yes. If the game is close and we need to win, no. Remember, we're in a play-off battle. I owe it to the team and the city to try to win every game. I hope the kid understands.

"I'm sure he does," I answered. "But will the rest of Chicago?"

The manager gave me a look that said that this is his team. The public will have to understand that. He doesn't run this team on a vote of the fans.

While I could agree with him, I also remembered the rowdy crowd at the game last night. The fans were in an emotional mood. The story had taken their imagination to a new level.

While Jason and the rest of the team bounded out on the field to do their stretching, I went over to my seat to soak up some of the late September afternoon sun. To my surprise Tim also came early to catch practice. "You're here a bit early. What brings you out this time of the day?"

Tim grinned. "I thought I'd just relax like you and catch a few rays. How's our guy doing?"

I told him about the conversation I had with Kowalski that morning and how impressed I was on how he handled all the adversity. "I don't know if I could have handed it."

Tim looked out on the diamond and said, "I think I understand Jason very well, you see, I went through something like he went through,"

So then Tim explained that he is a cancer survivor. A few years ago he had prostrate cancer and had gone through chemotherapy. He explained how difficult it was. How much pain and suffering he encountered. How weak he became during the treatment.

"Each day was a new adventure," he said. "There were days I didn't want to get up and go through another treatment. I did though, because I had a family and friends that needed me and I wanted to be with. I couldn't let them down and I couldn't let myself down.

He survived after the standard treatment and it has been 4 years since the last treatment. He's hopeful that he can hit the five-year mark. "I thank God everyday for this gift, I hope the gift lasts. If not I'll start all over again. I depend on my family and friends and they on me, That is the way it's supposed to be.

Well that was another mouthful for me to digest, but it explained why Tim got involved with this case. He saw something of himself in Jason and he wanted to help.

As the crowd was coming in, I could feel the anticipation of what they hoped would happen. The buzz was out; they hoped Kowalski would finally play today. They also wanted the Cubs to win. I don't think anyone realized that the two were not compatible with each other.

All over the stands were home made signs. Some read 'Good luck, Jason' others said 'Let him play.' The most inventive one I saw was one that simply said 'Free Kowalski,' yes, the crowd was ready for anything today.

As the lineup for the game was announced, there was a groan from the fans. I guess many of them still did not understand the rules laid down by the Commissioner. Then I heard something, which caused many of the fans to become further, dismayed. The Commissioner was to be in attendance for both games that weekend. I guess he wanted to make sure that the rules he had applied to Kowalski would be followed.

The game started with the Cubs taking an early lead of 3 to 0 after two innings. However, they couldn't maintain that advantage and soon the game was tied at 3 by the top of the sixth.

At the top of the sixth a close play at the plate came about. The Astro's runner was safe at home when he slammed into the Cub catcher and knocked him out cold. A fight ensued and both benches emptied. Of course, there was Jason joyfully ready to duke it out with any Astro that came near him. Luckily, one of the Cub players held him back and nothing happened.

When the dust settled and calm was restored, the pitcher for the Cubs needed to warm up a bit before the game started again. The new catcher wasn't ready, so the manager sent Jason out to do a little catching while everything was ready.

At first, the crowd didn't recognize Jason, Then someone shouted "its Kowalski!"

Suddenly the whole of Wrigley Field cheered en masse. The noise sounded like a jet plane. You would have thought Babe Ruth came back to the dead and called his home run shot all over again.

Almost as soon as it started Jason left the field and the crowd groaned again.

Many thought that that was it. This was Jason appearance on the field and the show was over,

The Cubs lost the game 5 to 4. They had to win tomorrow to remain tied for the last play-off spot. That meant that Jason would probably not get a chance to play with every good player needed.

The press crowded around Jason. "How did I do, guys," joking with the press. The reporters asked if his "appearance" satisfied the requirement to be part of one game? "I suppose so, I don't think they'll put me in as important game as there will be tomorrow."

The manager pulled me over to the side, "Kowalski is still a part of this team, until the end of the season, and I'll try and put him in as a pinch runner tomorrow. The Commissioner is not going to dictate how I run this team."

The manager noted that Jason's positive, loose attitude has been help in a tight play-off race. "His presence has kept the focus on him, rather than the team. That's what this team needed in the stretch run. He's here to the finish."

Looking at the players in the locker room, I could see that it was true. Despite the close race, the team was loose and not especially bothered by the press. It was a good sign for the coming days.

Of course he couldn't stay forever. Eventually he would have to leave if the Cubs got into the play-offs. After all, they would need every player they could have. With the extension of the roster in September, they could afford Kowalski, but the play-offs were a different matter. They would have to play with a 25 member play off team. They would no longer have the luxury of keeping Jason.

I could only hope the Commissioner feels the same way.

I asked Tim to take Jason home and he agreed. Then went back to my hotel and got ready to have dinner with my ex wife.

We arranged to meet at a pizzeria that used to be one of our favorites when we were first married. It wasn't for romantic reasons we decided on the place. Rather it was the most convenient place that we both knew. I wasn't so much apprehensive about seeing Brenda as much as I wondered why she was so insistent on us getting together.

When I got to the restaurant, Brenda was already there. As always she looked terrific. She had always taken care of herself. She was still the same petite gal I knew in college, though I suspected that her dark hair, was helped by a good bottle of hair dye. Of course, I should talk. Though I managed to still have most of my hair, I was pretty much gray, these days.

She greeted me with a kiss and a hug. I could tell, however, that she was more than usually nervous and maybe on edge.

"So, how's the story coming along?" she said as I settled in.

"Great, so far, Might be the best thing I have written in years."

We talked a while of old times, and how we came here often. I asked about the condo, and she told me that she had bought some new furniture, as some of the pieces were getting 'ratty,' as she put it.

Then it came time to ask, "What made you decide to call me. Couldn't the lawyers have handled it?"

She glanced down on her glass of wine, "Rob, I need your advice, as a friend. We still are friends, yet, right? Also as someone who has gone through something like this themselves."

"I think you better start from the beginning." I put down my coffee, leaned back and began to listen.

From there it all came out. Seems that on her watch a patient had died when he or she was given the wrong medication by one of her nurses. The family was planning to sue and the hospital, in order to minimize the damage had proposed that she, along with the nurse involved resign. Sounds familiar, right?

She told me that the hospital was insisting that she may be fired and perhaps it would be a good idea if she would resign, but at that point she was reluctant to do anything like that. "This job has been everything I wanted. I've given up a lot in staying here. Even to the point of giving up my marriage. I wasn't the one who caused the death, but because it was on my watch, they want me to suffer."

I could have laughed, but I didn't. Having been there and done that, I also knew how difficult it must be. I knew how hard it was to leave a job you loved. Like I said, I could have thrown it all back on her. Some would say it would serve her right. But after being around Jason and doing this story, I couldn't see myself playing the heavy any more.

I asked her what she wanted to do, "In your heart, do you want to fight, or just walk away. That's the question that only you can answer."

She said, "I'm the type that would rather fight. I put too much into my career to just walk away"

"Look," I replied. "Your case and mine are a little different. I couldn't find who did what to me and I was given almost no time to discover what happened. Sure, I could have stood up and fought. But I was given no time. I did what I thought was best at that time. You have the ability to see what could happen if you are forced to resign. You saw what happened to me. It's your choice; you have more knowledge than I did, then. It's what you feel you want that counts."

She looked at me and smiled. " I figured you would say something like that. But let me ask you, are you happy with the decision you made?"

I thought about it. I haven't always been sure that I would have done everything exactly the way that I did. I would have skipped the drinking. I would have done a better job search. I would have listened more to others, including Brenda. But, then I might have not been able to be a part of what I'm doing now. When it all comes down to pass, it's always a trade off. I could have been happy either way, I can't change the past nor can I predict the future. I could only live in the here and now. I was happy now, no sense in wishing for anything better.

I told Brenda, that and left it there. She seemed to understand, but did she? That was something that she would have to figure out for herself. Only time and experience would give her the answer.

After dinner we took a walk through the Loop. Even though I had been in town over a week, I had not taken a walk and checked out the old places that were a part of my professional and personal life only a few years ago.

Brenda and I laughed at the old times and it seemed to me we had become relaxed with each other. She even got up the nerve to ask me, "Do you think, after all of this, you might want to come back to Chicago?"

Walking through the Loop brought me back to the things I always loved about Chicago. The Magnificent Mile, Water Tower Place, Marshall Field were all a part of my past, not only with Brenda, but then, I was younger.

When I was growing up my family would take the South Shore to downtown Chicago. We would spend the day in the Loop. Visiting all the stores and have a nice lunch at a nice restaurant.

There was one restaurant in the Loop in particular that served the best spaghetti I ever had, Just thinking about it today can get my taste buds to salivate.

We would go to Riverview Park and ride on the rides and have a great time there. Unlike the somewhat sterile amusement parks of today, Riverview was a wonder of sight and sound. I always thought of it as superior to the parks of today.

Yet, something told me that those days were over. I had found another place to make some memories.

I thought about all those things and said, "I'm not sure. These last few days have been interesting and have sparked some of my old love affair with the city. But you know, I've been in Arizona for a couple of years now. I'm getting used to the pace, the quiet, the laid back attitude that I see out there. Here, everything is noisy, pressing and loud. I love this place to visit. But I would rather live down there. I'm happy there."

Did I note a little bit of disappointment in Brenda? I thought I did. But she wasn't ready to press me further on my thoughts. I guess I was being more emphatic than I had been in years.

The walk did me good. The weather was cool and bright. The

company was pleasant and the city was as it had always been, big shouldered and brash. But I realized it no longer was mine.

We ended our walk where we started, in front of the pizzeria. I kissed Brenda good night and we each got in our cars to go home. Somehow I felt that I would hear from her again.

During the night I dreamed that I was the baseball player playing for the Chicago Cubs. While at bat I had worked the count up to 3 and 2. When I looked at the manager he signed to me that it was my decision whether to swing away or not. The opposing pitcher wound up and threw the ball; the ball was coming and I…. Woke up. Now I'll never know whether my at bat was a successful or not. Was it a metaphor for life? I would think so.

In the morning I shaved and dressed early and was reading the paper when again there was a knock at my door. Thinking it was Kowalski again; I bounded up to answer it. When I opened it I found Jerry Morris, the catcher that the Cubs called up from Triple A Iowa.

All through the last couple of days, I had the feeling that I knew Jerry. I couldn't put my finger on it though. Jerry was about 28, short but stocky, a Yogi Berra type. He asked if he could come in.

I offered him some coffee that I had sent up and asked him what he wanted from me.

"You don't remember me then? He asked.

I told him I didn't although perhaps I had heard of him when I occasionally covered minor league ball.

"Figures, I was one of the people that you fingered in that steroid story you wrote about 5 years ago."

Now I remembered where I had heard his name. When discussing the findings with the investigators at the newspaper office that first day his name was mentioned as one of the people that I had fingered. Although at the time I had made it a point to present the evidence to the public at the time without mentioning names, I had forgotten that the names were given to baseball officials when I turned over my findings.

Maybe I forgot the names because I just wanted to forget the trauma it caused me and to others. I'm sure that's why I didn't remember him any more.

I told Jerry, "I'm sorry, more than you'll ever know. If it pleases you it ruined my career to the point I couldn't find a job for over 3 years. My marriage failed and now I'm working for a paper in Mesa, rather than a big shot reporter in Chicago. If there's any other way I can help you, feel free to ask."

Jerry waved me off. "I don't want anything, but I wonder if you know the whole story,"

I gave him one of my dumb looks, the type I had perfected for years. It comes in handy in a pinch, especially when I wanted to get some information from someone and I wanted him or her to open up. This time though, I really was dumb.

Jerry said I didn't know the half of it. "Do you know who your contact was?"

I know his name is Scott Miller and that he was once a ball player for one of the minor league teams."

"Then you don't know that Scott wasn't a very good player but happened to be married to the daughters one of the owners of a minor league team."

Jerry proceeded to tell me that he DID use steroids at that

time and so did the others. Scott was pressured to change the evidence after he had handed the evidence to me. The pressure came from his father-in-law, who wanted to protect baseball from a terrible scandal.

I was floored. After five years of doubting myself, I find that I was innocent of any wrongdoing.

Jerry than told me a little of his story. He was a kid dreaming of some day being a star on a major league team. It didn't matter what team, just as long as it was a chance to play baseball. "Now, I come from the area near Shea Stadium," he recalled, " So I was a Mets fan. I remember how my dad and uncles would talk about the Miracle Mets of 1969, how you had to believe. As a teenager I remember being at the game when Buckner let the ball go between his legs and the Mets beat the Red Sox for the World Series. All of my buddies and I were in heaven. We had our own miracle team, just as our fathers had their miracle in 1969."

Over the years, while growing up, Jerry played sports, especially baseball. He was good but a little on the small side. Yet he always made the teams because he had a desire to play, which sometimes overcame any obstacles that size might have diminished.

"By my junior year in high school, I was trying desperately to impress college scouts that I was good enough and big enough to play on any one of their teams."

My high school coach, who is really a good guy, but badly misinformed, suggested that I try some steroids to bulk up. "It won't hurt you." He said. "With your swing and contact, if you bulk up you might be able to hit the ball with more power and authority, get more home runs and get into the majors a lot quicker."

Not knowing the effects that we do now, he agreed. Within a

few months he had bulked up to such an extent that he hardly knew himself any more.

When the senior year season began he was crushing the ball farther than he ever did. His pick off throws to second would be whipping fast and base runners began to fear his arm heading into second base.

Obviously, the college coaches drooled over him and he signed with a powerhouse program on the west coast. No one ever asked if he was on any kind of medication. They all acted as if he was doing it all naturally. It was a "don't ask don't tell" policy.

He stayed there for two years when he decided to take an offer with the team that drafted him about the time he signed to play college.

He quickly shot up in the organization reviews and would soon be called up to AAA ball with the team.

Yet, there were times that he would wonder if the steroid use were beginning to affect him. There were times where he was cranky and surely with people. There were also times that he thought that his heart would go out of rhythm and he didn't always think as clearly as he one did.

Yet, as worried as he was, he couldn't just stop taking steroids, He was too close in getting into the big show, His goal almost reached, he was not about to change everything and ruin his chances.

So he would not consider that steroids were to blame. He just figured that he just needed to calm down, focus and get the rest he needed that everything would be all right.


There were a few times he decided to stop taking the drug. However, whenever he did, he noticed a definite decline in his strength. So he went back again.

About five years ago, while playing he had some type of seizure on the field. He recovered, but in the tests that were taken, his steroid use was discovered. He was released by the team and told that he needed to gat clean. A short time after that, the Cubs picked up his contract and decided to make him their salvage project.

I asked Jerry if he was clean. "Yep," he answered. "For five years now. The manager got the others and me help and I had to start back at single A, after the team that had rights to me dropped me. I got another chance with the Cubs, and had to start at ground zero. But, I worked hard and now at least for the month I made to the big show.

"I lost my power some," he laughed. "But I worked on my other skills and learned how to become a better hitter, not through overpowering the ball, but with improving my timing and hand and eye co-ordination. "I think I'm a better hitter for average than I ever was at any time in playing baseball.

The he grinned. "You'll never know who asked me to come and tell you all of this. Your buddy, Kowalski."

I could only laugh at that. I might have suspected Jason would do something like that. Apparently Jerry and Jason's locker was next to each other and they had become good friends, which usually happens with new players. It one-way for rookies to survive,

As Jerry and Jason became closer, Jerry told Jason of his steroid use and what had happened to him.

He also related what he had heard about me and how badly he felt about it. "Jason suggested that I come to you and tell you my story as a way of healing both myself and healing you."

"Thanks Jerry" was all I could say. I've been living with this for five years. It's great to get the monkey off my back. Now, to find my old source."

"I happen to know that too" Jerry was just full of news. "He's living out in the south suburbs. I guess the marriage failed and now he's working for an Independent Minor League team in the south suburbs.

He gave me the address and asked that if I go to see him, he wanted to go too.

I told him that it sounded like a good idea. After the game tomorrow he and I would meet up with Scott.

But today would likely be the big day for Jason. I wanted to be ready and finished breakfast and then got into my car to go to Wrigley Field. Jerry had some breakfast with me and followed me to Wrigley Field in his car.

The players were just coming in when we arrived. Everyone seemed relaxed, as the team got ready for pre-game warm-ups

Jason seemed the most relaxed of them all. I asked him if he thought he would play and he answered, "I don't think so, this is too important a game to let a walk on like me in the game. I would only be willing to go in the game was out of reach."

The manager heard that and said to Jason, "I'm glad you feel that way, because that's exactly what I'm planning. If the game is out of reach either way I'll put you're in. If it's close then I can't, OK?"

Kowalski nodded and went about his business of getting ready. Giving encouragement to the team and relaxing them. Even that was a plus for a team that was struggling to get in the post season.

Out on the field I felt the last warmth of the autumn sun; it was going to be a nice day for a game, not too hot, not too cold.

After warm up and practice the team left the field to the Astros. As the players relaxed Jason and I talked a little.

"I never had a chance to finish my story of the recovery, Will you be around after the game for me to tell you?"

I assured him that I would like nothing better. "Now you guys just go out and win this game!" I put my hand on Jason shoulders and said, "Thanks for every thing."

Kowalski nodded and gave thumbs up. "Here's looking at you, pops."

Just before the Cubs were about to take the field Jason gathered the team around and said, "I want to thank all of you for allowing me to be a part of the team. You treated me kindly, when there was no reason to. You guys are my heroes, whom I will not forget, ever. You have fulfilled my dream and I am proud of all of you."

Kowalski stood on the doorway and shook hands with each player as they filled out. When Jason walked out to the field, the team gathered around and gave him a round of applause and a cheer.

Jason stood near the third base line slowly looking over the playing field and the stands. I went over to join him. As he was gazing over the stands, he suddenly turned pale and kind of waved to someone in the stands. As he waved, he muttered underneath his breath, "Oh my God, it's Gail,"

I looked around, and then quietly asked," Where is she?" He pointed just to the left, in a box seat on the third base side. She was tentatively waving to Jason as we stared after her.

Yes, It was Gail. I had seen a picture that Jason had showed me in our conversations. She looked a little older, her hairstyle had changed, but you could make no mistake about it, it was Gail.

I poked Kowalski. "Get a grip on it, kid. We got a game to play. I'm sure there will be plenty of time to catch up with each other and talk. Keep your head in the game, you might still be playing."

Jason agreed and went to the dugout for the start of the game. Soon after, I took my seat with Tim in the stands and got my own surprise, Brenda was there. I looked at her and she came over. "I figured that I needed to see what all the excitement that you've been reporting is all about" then she giggled.

I got Tim up to speed with all the happenings and he just said, "Now the both of you are going to be loopy today, got to keep your head in the game," then he laughed.

The umpire called play ball  and the game was on.

This game was to be no pitching dual from the start. Both teams scored 3 runs in the first. Houston on 2 homeruns and the Cubs on a series of doubles. The third inning saw the Cubs catcher knocked unconscious on a play at the plate. The Cubs manager gambled by putting in Jerry Morris as the new catcher.


 His gamble paid off in the bottom of the third when Morris hit a grand slam home run after three consecutive walks by the Astros pitcher.

The Cubs scored a run in the bottom of the fourth. But the Astros tied it in the top of the fifth.

Both teams were going through pitchers like they were candy. Both managers used their bench in the struggle to capture the final play-off spot.

This time the fans began to forget all about Kowalski as they cheered the team on. I wondered what Jason would think of all of that. Then, I decided that he's probably too wrapped up in the game to think about the possibility of playing. After all, I did.

After a scoreless but tense sixth inning (both teams loaded the bases but could not score), the Cubs and Houston exploded for 3 runs in the seventh inning.

I looked at Gail at one point then, and noticed that as much as she was watching the game, she often watched the dugout. Jason had only been seen once since the game started, when he went out to high five Jerry, when he hit the grand slam.

Houston scored 2 more runs in the eighth, but the Cubs finally caught them when their big gun hit a home run to tie the game at 12 apiece.

The ninth inning became the pivotal inning for every one involved, in more ways than one. The Astros scored 2 runs that inning, when the right fielder could not catch up with the ball and crashed into the ivy. He was out cold. The stretcher was called out and he was taken to the hospital for a CT scan.

The Cub's manager called me over to the third base side. As I came over he said." I got to put him in."

"Jason?"

"Yep, That's right. I have no choice. I got no one left that can play except a pitcher or two and I might need them later."

"What about the Commissioner?"

"I'm not even going to ask, I said that the important thing is to win with what I have. Kowalski is what I have. I'll use him. And deal with the Commissioner later."

So Kowalski finally gets his chance to be in the game. But not what he was expecting.

The home plate umpire came over and said, "that's the most unusual conference I've ever seen, but what are you going to do?"

"Kowalski is coming in to play right field."

Jason grabbed a glove and was greeted by the roar of 39,000 screaming Cubs maniacs. Then, realizing what was happening drew its collective breath.

Luckily for the Cubs, Houston hit into a double play. Jason did not have to make a play on the field and the Cubs came up trailing by two in the bottom of the ninth.

In the bottom of the ninth, the Cubs tied the game on a two run homer by their center fielder. But they couldn't score the winning run; the game went into extra innings with the game tied at 14.

The first Houston batter in the top of the $10^{th}$ hit a triple into left field. Now the lead run was only 90 feet away. When the next two batters struck out, there was a sigh of relief from the drained fans. One more out to go and the Cubs could have a chance to win. So far, Jason had survived his time on the field.

Listening to the radio broadcast that a fan had turned on, I heard a fantastic report. Apparently the Commissioner angered that the Cubs had put Kowalski on the field attempted to leave his Skybox and go to go to the Cubs dugout to protest to the manager. Some frantic Cub fans barred him from leaving his luxury box. They held the door in so he couldn't get out. Looking up, I could see him waving his arms and mouthing what I'm sure was not kind words about the Cubs manager.

I thought that maybe the police would come and rescue the Commissioner. Then I thought better of it. No policeman would dare provoke a bunch of frustrated Cub fans. They have waited all these years for all the excitement that they are having now. No one, not a policeman, not the military or the president would want to come to the Commissioner's rescue. He was stuck and he was on his own.

The final out for the inning was up to bat. He worked the count to 3 and 2. The Cubs pitcher had no choice but to throw a strike. The Houston batter hit a towering ball that was falling fast in… right field.

Jason had to run a mile to reach the ball. Although Jason had been conditioning himself to run, I knew that he was not that fleet of foot. I thought to myself, "he'll never catch up to it,"

The crowd had abruptly become a silent witness to history. I glanced at Gail and she didn't even watch. Head down, she shielded eyes from the sight before her. I thought I heard Tom praying, "Lord, let him catch the ball…"

Jason kept running. Faster and faster the ball came back down. At the last second Jason lunged for the ball and…. caught it just inside the webbing of his glove! He fell to the ground but kept the glove up and held on to the ball.

Kowalski seemed as surprised as any one that he caught the ball. The crowd let out a collective roar and his teammates pounded him with high fives and hand shakes. The manager just kissed on the cheek. It would be the catch that would rival Willie May's World Series catch in 1954.

The first hurdle was over. The bottom of the inning was to follow. Jason was to bat first.

As Jason was set to bat in the bottom of the inning, I asked Tim what he thought would happen. Tim replied that he figured that the manager would let him bat and try to take a walk or strike out. "After all, he's batting in the top of the inning and if he strikes out there's still two outs. The way this game is going there would still be time to get the run that they need."

It sounded reasonable to me. As it turned out, Tim was right.

Jason took the first pitch, a fastball, high and outside for a ball. The next pitch was a curve, low and off the plate for another ball. The fans cheered his discipline at the plate so far. The next pitch was a fastball right down the middle for a strike. Then Jason actually fouled a ball on what looked like a weak swing.

With the count at 2 and 2, everyone wondered what he would do on the next pitch. It came outside and Jason almost swung at it, but checked his swing at the last second, now the count was three and two.

I remembered Jason's story when he was playing Little League. I was silently telling my self that Jason had better give up the walk strategy.

The crowd had been roaring on every pitch in Jason's at bat. Now, they grew silent as the deciding pitch was about to be thrown. I noticed that Gail was hiding her eyes again. She couldn't bear to watch. The Cub players were all standing and had their arms stretched out as if giving Kowalski a boost of power. The moment had come.

The Houston pitcher came set and threw. He had thrown a breaking ball that somehow did not break. Jason swung and hit a fair ball between second and first that just eluded the outstretched glove of the second baseman and dribbled out in shallow right field. Jason had just enough speed to get a hit!

At that moment the crowd erupted in a cheer so loud I'm sure it could be heard in every Major League ballpark in America. It was another shot heard around the world.

The first baseman for the Astros handed the ball to Jason, and then shook his hand. Kowalski called time and waved to the crowd and walked over to the third base stands and motioned to me. I came down to congratulate Jason and he handed me the ball. "I want you to have this."

"Jason, that's yours, you earned it," I protested.

"Hell" he countered. "I got the glove, I got the bat and I got the uniform to always remember this day. You believed in me from the start and supported me during the hearing and all. You deserve something from this day, I figure"

I was stunned and ashamed. I had come to Chicago with a chip on my shoulders and a bad attitude.  There were others I thought could have received this present. Yet, I was grateful that I had a change of heart. So I thanked him. Then I took the ball.

Jason trotted back to first and the game was on.

The first base coach talked rapidly to Jason and he nodded. I noticed that Kowalski did not take any kind of lead off. Being a worse kind of a rookie in that type of a situation the Cubs decided not to take any chances and kept Jason firmly on the base, so as not to be picked off.

I looked up at the Commissioner's box and I could see him looking down at me. I held up the ball and waved to him. Tim doubled over in hysterics and said, "maybe Kowalski should have given the ball to the to the Commissioner, he's going to need a peace offering. He could say this is for his stance as regards to keeping integrity in baseball."

I only said that if the Commissioner wants a commemorative baseball, let him get his own hit.

But, like I said the game was still on.

The next two Cub batters walked. I guess the Houston pitcher was frustrated after an amateur like Jason got a hit off him. A new pitcher was called in and the next batter came up.

At each base Jason did not leave the bag. He watched the third base coach, letting him decide when to advance. But with the next two batters getting a free pass it wasn't necessary.

It was Jerry Morris again. Houston knowing that Kowalski was slow of foot brought the outfield in for a play at the plate. With the count at 2 and 2, Jerry lofted a fly ball over the centerfielder's head. Pumping his arm in the air, Jason easily trotted to home for the winning run!

The crowd erupted in yet another cheer, louder than any previously. The Cubs players pounded both Kowalski and Morris as they celebrated the their victory. They celebrated with the fans as they slowly went down the tunnel and into the locker room.

As the manager and team entered the locker room the commissioner met them. He was not a happy man. I guess the loyal Cub fans finally let him out of his skybox and he ran down to the locker room.

Here's the exchange he had with the manager:

Commissioner: What do you think you were doing? He

wasn't supposed to play. I specifically forbade that!

Manager: What did you want me to do? I didn't have another position player left! Oh! I suppose I could have used a pitcher, instead, but the way the game was going I couldn't afford it!

Com: Do you realize what you're doing to the integrity of the game?

Man: Oh, come off it! This probably helped the image of the game more than any one act could have done. Allowing one person to fulfill his dream is like saying to any one, if you want to believe and work at it, you can do anything! If you don't want this to happen again, have the owners ban it. As of now, I did what was right for the team. I won it for them and for the fans in Chicago, not for you or your blasted integrity.

Tim, who had come with me to the locker room, spoke up. "Mr. Commissioner, the manager is right. The idea for baseball is to win and to do whatever he can to legally win. That's what he did. You can't say he didn't. Kowalski was part of the expansion of the Cub roster. He is legally able to play. Technically you can't stop it. You can suggest, but as long as the player is eligible, he can play. By the way, the Cubs signed Kowalski to a contract, so he is a player of good standing of Major League baseball. I had him sign a contract after the hearing last week, just to cover an event, such as this."

Sputtering, the Commissioner left. He had no recourse. The Cubs won the second time in one day.

The celebration went on noisy and profane, for a couple of hours in the locker room.

At a press conference outside Jason was asked a few questions:

Q: Did you think you could get a hit?

Jason: Not at all. Actually, it was the only ball I saw during the at bat and that's why I swung at it. The fastballs, I never even saw, but hey, what about that catch!

Q: I suppose you didn't see that ball?

J: Actually, I could see the ball, but I didn't think I could catch up with that. I guess I ran faster than I ever did. When I saw it in the web of my glove I was the most surprised person in the park.

Q. Now that you won the game, what are you planning to do now?

J: I'm not going to Disney World. I plan to go home and go back to work in the warehouse. I think I've had enough excitement for a while.

Finally, it was time to go. I told Jason we would meet later for dinner and finish our conversation on his recovery after his set backs. As we came out of the locker room and out of the players entrance, there waiting for him was Gail.

Jason stood transfixed for a moment, and then walked forward toward Gail. Gail looked shyly at Jason and said hello. "I was watching you play today, I thought you were pretty good."

Kowalski stammered, "Yeah it was a real treat being out there, but man, I was scared to death I was going to blow it!"

Gail laughed then got serious again. "I don't know how you have managed getting from the transplant to here, I don't know if I could have done what you have done today."

Jason just smiled shyly and whispered, "you find your center and then you stay there."

"Hey, Jason!" I called. "See you for dinner later?"

"For sure," then he gave Gail his arm and they walked out into the night.

As I was heading to my car, I saw Jerry Morris standing nearby. "Good game, huh? Now do you want to go see Scott Miller and finish off a perfect day?

"I think that would be a great idea. I'm on a roll anyway, so why not?"

So we got in my car and headed to Scotts place to finally confront the one person who had ruined my life.

We got to Miller's apartment within a short time. I noticed that his lights were on so I assumed he was home. Jerry knocked on the door as I stood behind him.

In a few moments the door opened and I recognized Scott immediately as he did me.

I barged in and sat Scott down, "Do you know what the heck you did to me?"

Scott's eyes bulged wide and he stammered, "Rob, you never will understand the kind of pressure I was under. The players were going to get the help they needed, and I didn't think the paper would do what they did to you,"

He continued, "You got to understand, I had a wife whose father was an owner of a team. If this story continued he would have been out of the league. I would have been out of a job. As it is, my wife and I divorced a couple of years later because I was so guilty about what happened."

"You could have contacted me," I countered, "I had to suffer because of your not being able to tell the truth. Baseball would have been better off facing the problem head on rather than hiding it."

Scott looked at Jerry "you got help didn't you? From what I saw today you'll be on a big league team for sure next year."

"That's not the point. Baseball could have opened up and helped others a lot earlier, if the original story would have been pursued." Jerry was obviously angry and was going to let Scott know.

"Tell you what I'm going to do," I decided. When I get back to Mesa, I'm going to write about what I have learned. Then, everyone, including you will have a chance to come clean. If you do not cooperate, I will make your life miserable. I plan to clear my name and you are going to help me." If that was a threat, then that's what I wanted it to be.

"But I could lose my job!" Scott was obviously afraid.

"Well, I will let people know that you were pressured and I'll talk to your boss, but that's all I can promise." Given my anger and hurt that was the best I could do.

Jerry questioned me, "do you really want to do that, and I don't think he deserves it."

I thought about it a minute and said, "well, enough people have suffered with this. As long as I get my name cleared, I think I can be a little generous."

Jerry shrugged his shoulder and agreed. Scott, after too many beers and being barely part of baseball for almost five years was terrified that we could change our minds and beat him up, readily agreed to the terms of the deal and we left him sobbing at the front door, more frightened than sorry.

On the way back to Chicago Jerry asked me if I thought we

had been easy on Scott. I thought not. "He's not really sorry, but leaning on him more would have hurt our cause. It would have made him more resistant. I'd rather let him have a little leeway and if he tries to cheat us in any way, we can get back at him. I'll talk to Tim, and, if it's possible and get him to sign a sworn statement."

That satisfied Jerry. He was for anything that could be done to keep steroids and other dangerous drugs out of professional baseball. He didn't seem worried that this kind of expose could hurt his chances at professional baseball. "I think it might help clean up the game. With the amount of publicity this could receive, I think any team that tries to block my playing would be seen as a hindrance to the sport and give it a black eye.

I couldn't help but agree, but I'll watch the story to its conclusion, so no one gets hurt.

Finally, it was celebration time. Jason would meet me at the restaurant were the team was celebrating their wild card victory. The party was in full swing when Jerry and I arrived. Everyone asked what took us so long and Jerry said that we had a little errand to run and that everyone will know in time. Everyone teased him and I, saying that my new found rise in stature will cause all to be wary as they all were with Jerry's bat.

I saw Jason at a table, still with Gail. Apparently they had been talking since they met in the parking lot. They told me what they had been saying.

Gail told me how sorry she was for hurting Jason when he needed him most. Jason again countered "but Gail I told you that you were right. In the long run I would have never been able to have and raise a family. I would have been more a burden than a joy to be with and I would have never wanted that for you."

"Besides," Jason countered, "I was the one that did the breaking up, not you."

Both related that Gail was once married, but had recently gotten a divorce, in part due to domestic abuse and that she had a son, now four who was the center of her life.

She had read my reports over the internet and the newspapers and when she realized that this was the same Jason that she had once loved, she took a chance and came to the game in hopes of meeting him once more.

All In all it was a successful day for both. I wished them luck and hope everything would turn out right this time.

At last Tim came in. I had invited him and his wife to dinner with us. After all, Tim wanted to hear Jason's story of how he finally recovered.

CHAPTER 24: JASON FINISHES UP

After the second major operation, I was clearly in bad shape. Much later I learned that the surgery took as long as it did because they couldn't find the area where the leak was coming from. They did discover that it was underneath my heart, a difficult place to find and repair.

But the doctors did a great job and now came the difficult recovery.

When I first became aware of my surroundings, I discovered that I could barely move. I'm the type of person who, one could say, is in perpetual motion. I always have something moving. Whether it a leg, a foot, an arm, it doesn't matter. If it's able to move it does.

So when I tried to move my legs, it was next to impossible. Even moving my arms and hands proved difficult. It's

135

amazing that things like that you take for granted. When you can't use them, you really miss them. I know I did.

Everyone kept telling me to stay calm and not try to rush things. As for myself, all I wanted to do was to get well enough to get home and finish recovering there. But I literally had to learn how to walk before I could do anything else.

Then there was the little matter of being able to breathe on my own and not be dependent on a respirator. Also, being able to swallow and eat was another worry.

First I had to go through one more surgery to place a trach for the respirator in my throat, rather than down my mouth and have a feeding tube put in my stomach.

After going through that last surgery, I felt like my Dad when he had all of this done to him before he passed away. There were times I wondered that perhaps my fate would be the same as his. To say that it frightened me would be absolutely true. It also made me angry. I wasn't planning on the recovery being so complicated or iffy. After all that waiting and the surgery and all, who can blame any one for being the way I was.

I still don't believe that I was depressed about it, now matter what the doctors said. I was plain mad. I was mad at myself, because I went through all of this, the pain, the tests, the treatments and all to end up tied down to a machine and not being able to eat. Any person who has ever had to have either knows what I mean. You cannot understand how it is until you have to go through the experience.

One of the hardest things to do at any time in a hospital is to sleep. With the noise and machines running to keep you going, it makes it difficult to get more than a couple hours rest. A lot of times it seemed that when I finally would fall asleep, someone would wake me up for something.

What really frosted me was the idea of the nurses and nurses' aids waking me up at 3 or 4 in the morning and giving me a bath. I think that it is one of the most ridiculous things I ever experienced. On top of that, this was the wintertime. It was cold and when the air hits a body that has been washed off and still wet, it is the worst thing you can do to some one recovering from major surgery as I was.

This was true in all the places I was in. at Loyola and the two rehab centers. I wouldn't have minded if it was before I went to sleep at night or say around 6 AM, but never in the middle of the night.

At Loyola it wasn't too bad, although it was difficult. One of the major things I had to accomplish was being able to breathe on my own. Now, I'm a shallow breather. After all my old heart caused my lungs to have a more difficult time. So to save breath I had automatically learned to breathe shallow. Now a machine was helping my lungs, it made things easier. If I wanted to get out on my own and out of the hospital however, I had to learn to breathe on my own.

I will say that the staff and nurses were helpful and kind. For the most part my stay there was good. But I still was not making much progress. My doctors decided to move me to a rehab center were they had good luck in getting people off a respirator.

If sometimes things don't make sense, it's because my sense of time is messed up. After about six weeks at Loyola, I was transferred to the other rehab center.

Don't ask me how the food was at the first rehab center. I never had any, due to the tube feedings. One problem I had was the fact that I was on continuous feeding. Which made me uncomfortable all the time. I don't know if it was the formula they were giving the amount, or me but while at the rehab center, I had severe cramps. The worst I ever had. I complained to the nurse taking care of me and they and me cut the amount they were giving me and the rate they were feeding me. Immediately, I felt better.

They were fairly successful in starting to wean me off the respirator. I was breathing on my own for six hours. More than I ever was at Loyola.

I still had trouble sleeping. The unit was set up as a giant ward. There were no doors to the area where I was staying. So the noise from the nurses and the techs could be heard trough the night.

Also, I didn't like one respiratory technician, who insisted on suctioning me every two hours, whether I needed it or not. There were times where she would do this when I was sleeping at night. This is not a good idea. How would you like to be wakened up by having someone put a suctioning tube down your throat? Most of the time after waking up with that happening, it was hard to fall asleep. By the time I did fall asleep again, she was going through the whole thing awakening me again. I asked her to not do the treatment, if I was asleep, but she ignored me.

The third night she did this. I stayed awake. When she came around again for the next treatment, I closed my eyes as if asleep. When she reached for the tube on my neck to suction, I reached for her hand, grabbed it and said, "Don't ever come to do a treatment when I am sleeping. If you do it again I will report you." She never bothered me when I was sleeping. I must have scared the living daylights out of her. Like some people say, you have to watch everything and if they are not doing what is right to help you say so. It is their job.

Just before the doctor at the rehab center was going to see if I could stand to be totally off the respirator, I developed jaundice and I was taken back to Loyola for treatment and to find out why the event occurred.

That meant another setback. I was kept on the respirator and had to start all over in getting weaned off the respirator.

After a week at Loyola, I was put in another rehab center. There are times I considered it more like a prison than a place to get well. I won't blame anyone individually for not trying, however, I know that they didn't know how to treat anyone who had a transplant. It certainly showed.

I was still on tube feeding and eventually was given a clearance to eat food. I thought I had the clearance when I was at Loyola, but they insisted that they had to run their own tests and I had to wait. When I was finally cleared, I almost wish I wasn't. The food was terrible. They also insisted that I continue the tube feeding. With my bowels not able to function well due to inactivity. I always felt stuffed. I looked like I was about seven months pregnant.

When I asked to get off the tube feeding, the nutritionist refused and insisted I both eat and continue the tube feeding. I insisted I could not do either. "It's like putting Chicago into Providence, Rhode Island. It can not be done." My pleas fell on deaf ears.

They did however cut back on the tube feeding; I was only on it about half the time than previously. That did help some. But, of course the food was so bad I thought that it might have been better on the tube feeding.

So I just threw away part of my meals, when ever possible. That way everyone would be happy. It worked, I don't believe that anyone ever suspected. Except since I didn't gain much weight. I would think they would wonder.

I was doing well again with getting off the respirator. Then I had a problem. My red cell counts were low at times. To get it back up to normal level, I would occasionally get a blood transfusion. One time I received a blood transfusion and somehow had a bad reaction to it. It seemed that I got the wrong blood type and had a bad reaction. Suddenly, I couldn't breathe and my heart rate shot up sky high. After what seemed forever getting someone to come and help. I was immediately put back on the respirator and had to stay on it for a number of days. I would have to start all over again.

Days turned into weeks and weeks turned into months. Sometimes it seemed that I would never get better. At one time, for after receiving the wrong dye for a CT Scan, my kidneys shut down. So, I was put on dialysis for one session.

For any one that has never been on dialysis, I hope you never have to go on it. While I know that it can be a lifesaver for many, it is a hard treatment. It takes a lot out of you. From the time they put in the tubing, in my case, through the thigh, to the treatment itself I felt wrung out. I had only one treatment. I was glad it was only one.

Between all of these things, I also had rehab sessions of walking in the morning and afternoon and another rehab session in trying to learn to take care of myself.

The two therapists that came to see me were good, but overworked. The sessions were only about 30 minutes in length, but I did try to sit up in a wheel chair as much as I could. It wasn't easy with having to deal with the respirator and all the tubing I was still hooked up to.

Most of the time, except for the staff that came into the room and my family and friends that came to see me. I had no contact with any of the other patients (I had a private room), except for one person. Let me tell you the story:

As I said, I had physical therapy twice a day for thirty minutes. The therapist, Hank, was a good guy, but like Sue, the occupational therapist, completely overworked. They had to take care of; I would guess ten to twelve patients a day.

That meant not only going through the exercises, but also writing reports for each person they visited. Then there were the patients like me, crabby, tired from all the nurses and other therapists coming in 24 hours a day, interrupting your sleep at night. Washing you at 3:30 in the morning and so forth.

Poor Hank, especially for the afternoon session! Most of the time I would be sleepy after being up for seven or eight hours, most of the time in my wheel chair. I would ask to get to bed for a little while in the afternoon and usually fall a sleep.

When Hank came, he would wake me up to start another round of walking down the hall. I'm crabby when I first wake up in the morning when even I feel good. Imagine how I was when I felt like the lint inside a coat pocket! I would have rather slept, but no, I had to get up and move around. Not the best way to get on my best side.

Each day I struggled through the walking sessions. I know that it was as frustrating for Hank as it was for me. If there is one thing or person who got me through the whole thing was one patient.

When I took my walk with Hank, there would be two ways to go. One way was toward the main entrance, then toward the small gym where the occupational therapy was done. The other route I took was toward the sunroom at the far end of the hall. There I could sit down and rest and have a look outside. Sometimes Hank would sit and talk with me for a bit. Then there were times he would check on another patient that he was doing some rehab with. After a while, he would come back and get me and I'd start the long walk back to my room and get ready to sit until dinner and then get set up for bed.

Occasionally, I would maneuver my wheel chair to where I could look out. That was difficult to do since I was hooked up to the respirator and I could only go so far. For me it was better than just watching TV, I did enough of that any way.

Occasionally, I would see Hank, walking another patient. He was a tall, lanky black man. He seemed to walk with a decided limp and as always, Hank would follow him with a wheel chair and a tank of oxygen, as Hank did with me.

One day, in June, I believe, Hank came for our session and again we started our long walk. A lot of times Hank would let me pick the direction that we would go. Usually, I would pick the direction of the sunroom. I enjoyed being able to look out and see the weather and a little bit of green, or at least what greenery that existed around the rehab center, which wasn't much.

That day, Hank asked me to sit for a while, he had to see about another patient, I told him fine and he left.

I proceeded to just look out the window and relax for a bit. A short time later, I was interrupted from my reverie; by Hank bringing the man that I had seen so many times walking the floors, just like he saw so many times.

I noted that besides being tall and lanky, he was much older than I had thought, about his middle fifties. You could see that he was tired from the walk, but he also seemed to be glad to be out.

He came over to me, held out his large hand and said, "Hello, my name is John Henry. Some of my friends who know me well call me Old Dude."

I laughed at that. "Well, I'm not called any thing but Jason Kowalski. I've might have been called a lot of things behind my back, but for the life if me, I never found out what they are."

He laughed at that one. Hank said to me, "I didn't know you

142

had a sense of humor." I told Hank that up until that moment lately, I wasn't sure if I had lost my sense of humor or not and that it was good that I found it again.

John Henry continued. "I've seen you walking these halls in the last few weeks and I asked Hank who you were, and what your story was."

I was surprised and maybe a little ashamed. I had seen John Henry out and about on his walks and never thought to ask who the heck he was. Maybe I had become too closed to people during all this time of isolation, both before the transplant and during the recovery.

"Well, young dude," said John Henry, winking at me. "I thought that since we're both stuck in here together, we might as well get to know each other."

I was surprised and maybe just a little bit embarrassed. I'm the type of person that gets to know people slowly before I relax and let my hair down with them. So when someone come up to me and puts out the glad hand, I tend to be cautious.

Hank got another chair for John Henry and told both of us that he had to go take care of something else and left.

John Henry sat down and looked me squarely in the eye and said, "So, I hear you are a heart transplant patient that you have had a hard time of it during your recovery,"

I noted that his speech was very precise, very educated. I figured that he had gone to college somewhere and had acquired a great education.

"Yes, I did out east, in New England," He laughed at my very stupid question. "If you want, I could talk some black English."

I apologized. "No, No, just keep what your doing, it's my fault if I have some things to learn,"

"Good." He looked at me again with that insistent look. "You haven't answered my question, having a tough time aren't you?"

I told him what was bothering me and how I felt about everything, I had not been that open with anyone in along time.

For himself, he just listened, nodding his head as I talked. Letting me know that he was listening and understanding every word I was saying.

We talked for about an hour. Hank came back for us, but seeing that we were enjoying the talk and company, he just left us there to continue our conversation.

At one point I dared to ask him why he was here.

First he raised his leg of his pajama bottom to reveal that his right leg was artificial. Then he told me what happened.

"Years ago, probably before you were born, I was a standout basketball player for the University of Connecticut. I played point guard and was a good one. I wasn't a dummy, like some other athletes. I studied hard and got a degree in History and a minor in Secondary Education.

Our team did fairly well, but not great, at that time the NCAA Basketball Tournament wasn't like it is today. A lot of NBA scouts loved me and I was drafted by the Chicago Bulls in the second round of the draft right out of college.

A short time after the start of training camp, I was walking home from the grocery store and was hit by a car. The driver was drunk and driving with out a license.

As for my self, my leg was crushed. The doctors at the hospital worked mightily to save the leg. They almost succeeded, but an infection set in. It was three weeks after the accident that my leg was amputated just above the knee.

My basketball playing days was finished, but not my dreams. After doing rehab work, I went back to Connecticut and landed a job teaching and coaching freshman basketball. Soon I ended up as the head basketball coach for the high school. My teams won three state championships in the twenty years of coaching.

I'm proud of that record. Not as proud as I am in all the students that I helped get a good education and went on to college. I insisted on that even to those that were in my basketball program. I wanted them study hard and mot just rely on athletics to make it in the world.

If they had any doubts I would just show them my wooden leg and tell a little of my story. That usually got them thinking. Not many of them took their lessons lightly. All of them have done well in school and I'm proud of all of them."

Before I realized it. The nurse came and said that we had to go back to our rooms and have our dinner. It was 5 pm. We had been talking for nearly three and a half hours. As the nurses took us back to our rooms, John Henry turned to me and said, "Tomorrow, how about we take our walk together, for our therapy?" I told him that that was a great idea and I looked forward to it.

That night after all I had done, I was exhausted. I slept well that night. Even the nurses were surprised. I even slept through the feeding as I finally got a good day of activity in.

The next day, about 1pm Hank came to my room and was surprised that I was ready to go. Outside the room was John Henry, As I slowly walked out the room, he said to me, "I see we have to work on your speed, you'll never make my

145

basketball team with those legs," I had to admit that I had a long way to go if I ever was going to play any kind of sport again.

As we walked first to the front entrance then back to the sunroom. I noticed that John Henry had never mentioned why he was there at the rehab center. When we sat down and began another talk, I asked him point blank. My asking might have surprised him, because it certainly surprised me. But he answered me straight away.

"Cancer" he said, and then smiled wanly. "Believe it or not, I didn't smoke, but I got lung cancer anyway. One of my wife's nephews is a doctor. When the cancer was found and chemotherapy did not work, he suggested that I come out here and have the lung removed.

At that point Yolanda, his wife came into the room. She was living with her nephew's family while John Henry was in rehab.

"So, you're the young man that my husband was talking about on the phone this morning, I'm pleased to meet you.

She was about 48, I would say, tall and on the thin side, She had been a teacher at the same high school were he taught and soon fell in love. She also continued to teach math until the cancer problem and retired with John Henry, to take care of him at the time he needed her most. They seemed to make a perfect couple.

We spent the afternoon talking again, Obviously I had to tell my whole story again, but I didn't mind. It seemed to me that the more I told my story the more I discovered things about myself. Some things I liked and some things I didn't.

As I was lying in bed, that evening, after another long day, John Henry came in my room and asked if I was too tired to have some company. He was bored and not too sleepy and just thought if I wanted a little company, he would be glad to oblige.

Well TV was boring and I didn't think any one was coming to visit that night, so why not?

"Good," said John and then he pulled out a deck of cards, and started to shuffle the deck. "Do you know how to play Texas Hold 'em?

"No, I don't, just five card stud." I apologized.

John just sighed' "Well that 's for kids he said "But it will do for starters."

Now, we didn't bet for money and I'm glad we didn't make it strip poker; I was only wearing a hospital gown. So we played for toothpicks. I wasn't much good or John Henry was just plain lucky, put you might say I lost my shirt.

Finally the nurses chased John out and get me situated for bed. It was another night for sleeping well.

The next few days John and I continued our walks. He knew a lot about sports, especially basketball. And I knew a lot about baseball. That way we learned a lot about each other's sport. Time passed quickly and the days spent at in the hellhole as each of us called the rehab center. We were nice about it in front of Hank and Sue, but between ourselves, we thought the place had a lot to be desired.

The one thing that we both hated was the food. I couldn't eat much of it, in part, because of the feeding tube. Being out with John gave me a chance to be away from it. John said I was lucky. I could always say the feeding tube made me too full to eat much.

I told him guess again. They insisted that I eat a full meal, on top of the tube feedings. "Eat this slop?" he said. "You got to be kidding!"

I told him it was true. This was while sitting in my room waiting for dinner. I told him I wouldn't mind if the menu varied a little, but that was the worse part. It was the same slop every day.

About that time our meals arrived. Looking at it wasn't going to make it go away so we started eating.

John Henry could see that I was trying but my heart wasn't in it. Finally he said this is too much for anyone to eat, especially when it isn't good. Then he took some of what was on my plate, put it on a napkin and threw it out in the contaminated garbage can that they used to put some of my diapers, that I occasionally wore,

"That will take care of your problem." Then his voice got real low and he said to me, "next time you can't finish any this slop or it's too much for you, just do what I did and throw it out. The nutritionist doesn't have to know. She's a nut any way. What she doesn't know won't hurt her and it will probably save you."

So I took his advice. It seemed to work.

There was a time one evening that I was hearing guitar music coming from John Henry's room. It was blues guitar, some of the best that I ever heard. I asked one of the nurses if they could get me across the hall and listen for a little while. They sort of doubted whether the idea was good, but I insisted.

After getting me set up, I wheeled myself over to his room. John was surprised, bit happy. There he showed me how he learned how to play. Playing a little Howlin' Wolf, and later Blind Lemon Jefferson, I could see that he had been playing for a long period of time.

He told me what it meant to be able to master something like a guitar. "It gave me confidence. It gave me piece of mind, especially through all those times in my life when things were tough. I could imagine myself like BB King, or Albert King, or any of the other great blues guitarists. They had something to say, and said it through their music."

He continued "I'm educated, you know and proud of it. But, like anyone I like to know where I came from and be able to think about my ancestors and what they went through to get me where I am today. Playing the music of the folks before me gives me a connection to them."

I couldn't help but agree we need to know where we've been, to know how we got there.

I suppose that the staff would cringe when we got together, It seemed that we came up with so many ideas to pass the time.

After a while we were getting bored with just doing our daily walking routine. One day in the middle of the walk I noted how boring it was. John turned to me and suggested, "Why don't we race? "I looked at him as if he was crazy. He said "it's simple, we just see who can make it to the sunroom in the shortest amount of time. No pressure or any thing like that, just to see who can get to the end first."

So that's what we did. With the help of Hank and his assistant to follow with the wheel chairs, we started from my room to the front entrance and then to the sunroom. The only restriction was if one got a little tired both would stop and rest until the other was ready to go again.

At go we began. At first John Henry was in the lead, mainly because he could walk faster. However, I slowly caught up, because I had more help and slightly better lungs. Both of us had to rest a few minutes, but we both made it in about a half an hour. In the end I had perhaps a two- foot lead when we came to the sunroom. Hank and his assistant called it a tie mainly because one or the other would have had to let the other in the sunroom first, because the doorway was not big enough for two to fit through.

As I was starting my last time getting weaned off the respirator, John Henry came over one day with Yolanda bringing a combination TV and VCR. "I got something I want to show you," as usual in that precise language that he often used. He then popped in a tape.

On the screen was a younger and more athletic John Henry, playing basketball for his college. He was good, very good in fact. I could see why he was picked in the NBA draft. His moves were graceful; his scoring touch was right on.

You could tell that John Henry really missed his ability to play, but as he explained to me that there were other trade offs in not being a basketball star. "I would have never have met my wife or had three state championships. Most important, though, I would have never have been able to see and help so many good young kids." When you get an opportunity to do something, to expand on what your dream is, don't hesitate go after it. No matter how large or small it might be."

Feeling tired, John said that he thought he would go to bed. Then he said that he wanted to see me off that 'damn' machine and start my way back home. That I had stayed at the rehab center long enough.

The next day Hank came in the morning for my late morning walk. As we got outside in the hall I asked where John Henry was. "Let's go toward the sunroom, I got to tell you something, Jason." Hank seemed serious.

When we got to the sunroom I sat down, Then Hank pulled a chair out and sat down. "I got to tell you something, Jason. John Henry had a bad time of it last night and he had to be taken to the hospital. It seems to be pretty serious."

He told me that he had told the staff not to tell me last night, since I was sleeping so well and I needed to be as strong as possible to get off the respirator.

Well the next few days were good as far as getting off the respirator, but it was a little lonely without my friend keeping me entertained while I got off the respirator. But I succeeded. It would been nicer to have been able to share my good fortune with John Henry as well my family, but in some way I think John Henry would know.

As I was getting ready to get out of the rehab center I was waiting for the final ok to get out there.

I heard a cough and saw John Henry's wife Yolanda, at my door. She came in and smiled to see that the respirator was gone. Then she said. "Jason, John Henry died last night. Before he died, we talked. He made me promise to come and give this gift to you and to tell you how glad he was to have you as a friend and making his last days some of the happiest that he had during this last long Illness."

The she handed me the VCR tape that we had watched the last time we had been together. She then bent over and kissed me on the forehead and quietly walked out of my room.

When I was finally released and everyone was gathering my stuff together, I told him or her to hand that tape over to me, that I would take care of it. I held that tape all the way back to the next stop on my journey home. If there were anyone that I could thank for getting me out, it would be John Henry.

Yes, I made up my mind to get off the respirator and get out of the place. I was mad and I was determined. I also had a friend like John Henry to help me get through the hard times.

Like I said before, I tried to use my anger to motivate me to get out of there, I was tired of looking same walls and the same people. Not that all of them were bad, but there was something more that I wanted to do. I would not be able to do any of it, tied down to a machine here,

First it was 2 hours than 4 than 8 hours. It was difficult. I hated the kind of system they were using. I could see that it was working. I didn't like the kind of trach collar that they used, but I had to work with what I was given. With no choice, I was managing. Soon I reached 16 hours. The next time it would be 24 hours and if I could reach that level, I would be free.

That early morning it began. I went through the day in good shape. Soon I reached the 16-hour mark. The next 8 hours would tell the story. I was even able to sleep well. Before I knew it I was at the 24-hour mark. I had succeeded.

The next few days were the best I felt there. In a few days I had the opportunity to go to another rehab center, near where I lived, I was on another leg on my long trip back home.

Finally I had another ambulance trip. This one though was back near where I lived. This was a relatively newer place and one where they worked as a team rather on an individual basis.

You got to deal with more people, patients and staff, everyone here had a smile and didn't act like the patient was a burden, but rather as a person of worth. They took the feeding tube out and gave me decent food. Soon I was eating 100% better than I was before and my stomach went down with much less gas than I had in months.

I got back to doing things for myself. With encouragement from my therapists and staff, soon I was walking around with a cane and washing myself with little problem. I was off of oxygen for what seemed like the first time since forever and toward the end of my stay had the trach tube removed.

After about seventeen days at that rehab center, I was ready to go home. Talk about being excited. I waited for my mom and a friend to come get me. After waiting for eight months, I couldn't get out fast enough. The nurse gave me the final instructions and I was released. Getting into the car and riding through familiar sights was exhilarating. As I got to my house, I saw my car. Just to see it did me good, even if I couldn't drive it.

Finally, I got into the house and as I did, I raised my arm up to give thanks to God, my dad and all those 'up there' that guided me through the long strange trip back home.

The next few months at home was spent on getting myself stronger. I started this round of therapy by working with a couple of therapists both occupational and physical. I would say I spent about four to six hours a day working out and doing my exercises.

I still couldn't walk much, at least not with out a cane. And I needed to get more upper body strength. So I worked on it. The best thing was that I was in my own home. That made all the difference in the world.

Each day I was doing more and more. I walked around the house several times a day and started using some small weights to get more strength. Within a month I was able to walk up the stairs and then get used to living in my own part of the house and working on the computer again. That was a major step to be able to do that.

Then I dared to drive my car, I found out I wasn't quite ready yet. In a parking lot someone was coming too close to me and I hit a pole trying to get out of the way. It was a minor thing but I waited a bit longer to get behind the wheel. When I did I started around my neighborhood, then expanded, as I got more comfortable. Soon, I was able to drive pretty easily and felt my sense of freedom coming back.

The last thing I had to do was to get rid of the cane. In February, about five months after getting home I had to go out and had forgotten my cane. I thought about going back and getting it. Then I thought I must not need it if I could just walk out of the house without it. So I continued on, I finished the whole trip without the cane, with that, I knew I had come back pretty well.

Without the cane I could walk pretty well. I started a walking exercise program that was pretty ambitious. I wanted to be able to walk two miles without interruption. I started by walking in the house, using a pedometer and checking my time.

My goals were too walk outside and try to do it within a half an hour. It took me about a month but I made it. These days I have cut it down to about 29 minutes. It's fantastic! What I really like is the walks I do around the neighborhood.

This is especially true during the summer months; It's a real gas to get out in the morning and just walk through the neighborhood. A lot of times people are not home due to work and all. But many are also out watering or cutting their grass. Some are pulling their weeds in the garden. Some even are just out on their porch taking in the early morning rays and enjoying a nice cup of coffee.

I usually walk down to the parish church, through the parking lot and down the next street and home again. Sometimes I just walk the four-block area around my home. I figure about 3 1/2 times end up as two miles. I especially enjoy it during the spring and fall. The air is cooler and usually fresh. That's when I do my best time. The summers are a little harder. It's a little too humid to go full steam. I'm usually about thirty seconds slower. I don't fret about it as long as I feel good after a walk; I figure I'm doing all right.

After a walk, I like to sit a little on the back the back porch and check out the trees and garden. We have a little garden in the back where we grow a few vegetables. I check on their progress and maybe even pick a few that are ready before getting back in the house.

I don't stop in the winter or when the weather is bad. There are always the shopping malls. Those are always fun. I enjoy it early in the morning, before the stores open up. There are other walkers there. A few times they see the pace I'm going as ask if they can join me. I tell them sure, but also let them know it's all right to slow down. Most of the walkers in the mall are older people and I realize that I might be doing a walk that they are not used to.

If I see that someone cannot keep up, I sometimes slow down. I don't feel that I should try to show up any one. Sometimes I think that if they feel that they can keep up with me, it makes their day and gives them something to brag about when they get home and see their relatives or friends.

I can just hear them now. "Hey, I can keep with this young punk during our walk. Bet you can't do that." If it makes them feel good about themselves for a little while why not?

When I was in the last rehab center I did the same thing. Toward the end of my stay I was doing quite well. Not perfect mind you, but pretty good. Around me there were others that were not as well. These were mainly older individuals. I didn't feel like show showing them up. By that time I was able to do such things as catch and throwing a ball pretty good. I was usually catching and throwing the ball off my fingertips. I was becoming a regular Michael Jordon.

Occasionally, I would miss a throw or two just to make things interesting. I felt that some of the older less active ones in the group would feel that they were less intimidated if they saw that I could occasionally miss a throw or catch. The staff recognized what I was trying to do and appreciated my efforts.

CHAPTER 25: ROB AGAIN

As Jason was telling his story, more and more people at the restaurant had gathered around to listen. There were members of the team, patrons of the restaurant and employees. He kept us captivated for almost two hours.

Yet, all through the tale he never thought himself special. For as he said. "I'm just telling you what happened. There were probably times I was the worst patient you could have. I generally like to do things for myself. To have to depend on others is a terrible feeling. You have to learn how to surrender. There my be times that you may lose your independence, but that doesn't mean that you have to lose your dignity."

After that, the party was over. The players each congratulated themselves once more and reminded each other that the play-offs were next.

For Jason, it was the end of the road. As of tomorrow, he will become Jason, the warehouse employee again. Not, as he put it, "a small cog in the baseball machine."

CHAPTER 26: THE NEXT DAY

That morning I called my editor from my room and told him about the encounter I had with my old source Scott. He laughed. "I can see you being the heavy, on second thought, no I can't. But you have a good story here. It will set the baseball world on fire. We'll go with it."

Then I suggested that I let one of the stringers handle the main reporting. It would write a piece on how I discovered the information and maybe interview Jerry.

"The kid's a stringer I know, but Perkins has a lot of enthusiasm and I want to give him a chance on a big story."

I knew Perkins a little. Always hanging around, making a pest of himself with his enthusiasm and persistence. He was a skinny little kid who walked with a limp from polio. But he seemed smart and eager to please. I figured he would be the perfect one to do the main story.

I called him and told what had happened. He was excited to no end. This was his chance and he was eager to make the most of it.

I went further, I told him that if the story would be any good, I would let him have the first interview with Jerry and possibly me on a background story. I figured that someone else writing the story would be better than me. It would adhere to journalistic standards.

Before I left the hotel I sat down the last story on Jason and his playing in that final game:

KOWALSKI GETS MORE THAN HE WISHED

Chicago__ Jason Kowalski lived the American Dream yesterday. With one small swing of the bat, he entered the annals of legendary baseball players.

Getting a lead off single in the bottom of the $10^{th}$ inning. He set the stage for a rally that gave the Cubs a 15-14 wins over Houston. Scoring the winning run, Kowalski helped the Cubs get into the play-offs.

The hit was not with out controversy. The Commissioner of baseball charged the Cubs with ignoring a ruling he had made just a few days before. Then, he had allowed Jason only the opportunity to pinch run and not take the field as either a position player or as a pinch hitter.

The manager having run out of players in the ten-inning slugfest had no choice but to play Kowalski. Jason rewarded the Cubs manager and his teammates with a shoestring catch in right field and then a softly hit single between first and second in the bottom of the tenth.

It was reported that the Commissioner went to the Houston manager, urging him to protest the game, where he would uphold the protest and thus give the game to the Astros.

The Houston manager refused, saying that the hit was legitimate. "Our pitcher reported that his breaking ball had slipped and he did not throw an easy pitch to Kowalski.

It was also learned that Kowalski was signed to a baseball contract as a legitimate player, with all the rights to play the game, as his manager would see fit.

Jason was asked how he was approached when it was decided that he would play.

"The skipper called me over to him and said that he had no choice that he would have to let me take the field. I asked him about the ruling from the Commissioner and he said to let him worry about that. He needed me to finish the game and get this team into the pay-offs.

Thee injured right fielder called me to the locker room and told me that I had to do it. He then gave me his glove and gave me the thumbs up. So I went out and did the best I could.

The rest of the story is history.

I like happy endings. This on certainly had a happy ending. It seems that baseball has won again. In it's over 100 years of existence, we have had many examples of courage and heroics, This game yesterday was no different then those games. A man comes up with a hit and we are changed. Tomorrow it will be someone else. But it will in no way diminish what has occurred here.

A man got a hit and won the game.

---

Then I packed the rest of my stuff and checked out of the hotel. I then drove to Wrigley Field to see Jason for the last time.

As I got to the park I found Jason packing his belongings from his locker. The rest of the team was getting ready to practice for the next game in the next couple of days. I suggested a walk around the field for the last time, the manager said ok, so we went out.

It was a cool, gray day. The first real hint that fall had arrived. The ivy, once green and flowing, had begun to look old and brown. Soon the leaves would be falling down. Hopefully after the Cubs played their last game of the season.

When I was younger, I remember seeing pictures of Wrigley Field in the winter. It always seemed so cold and barren. It actually seemed to me that the place was calling out "come on, let's play some ball, I would love to have some company."

I asked Jason if he ever felt that way. "Every year I do. The longest time of the year is the time between October and April. I hear some old time players felt like they were dead during that time and only came to life again, when spring training started."

I couldn't have agreed more.

We went back to the locker room to say good-bye. The players, each one, stepped up and wished Jason good luck and thanks for being a part of the team. The manager thanked him for coming through in the last game. "You made my gamble pay off, though I had a feeing that you wouldn't let your team mates down.

Then it was out through the tunnel and out the players exit. We walked quietly through the parking lot to our cars. When we got to mine Kowalski turned and said, "Well, I guess this is it."

Jason said to me, "You know when I have kids and when I have a chance to tell my nephews and nieces about all that happened this past week, they are going to look at me and say. Na, it never happened. It's just a story, a fantasy."

I shook my head " you don't have to prove any thing. If they question your truthfulness, all you will have to do is bring out the old Bill James Baseball Encyclopedia and point out the page with your name on it. It'll say Kowalski, Jason, Bats right, throws right, At bat 1, Hits 1, put outs 1. Then, every one will have to believe you."

Jason smiled. "So every fantasy is a reality and every reality is a fantasy, it just depends on your point of view,"

"Yep, I suppose so." What else could I have said? I had been through an experience that had changed how I looked at baseball and how I looked at life. Without realizing it, I had been affected in ways that I still do not understand.

Tim came walking up to us. "You didn't think I would let you two leave with out saying good bye, did you?"

Tim shook each of out hands and said so long, but not good-bye. "I don't think you can never say good bye to something or people like this."

He told Jason that if he needed any legal concerns to give him a ring. "After all, you think this is over? There will certainly be people who will want to hear your story. They'll want interviews, exclusives and endorsements. I might be able to help. If you want it."

We thanked Tim and since everything was said that needed to be said, we each went tour cars and drove off.

I got on my flight at Midway Airport. As we took off I suddenly recognized that I could not go home any more. The ten days I spent in Chicago was great but I was glad to get back to the quieter life in Mesa. I was set to get back to the heat, the gila monsters and the unending sun. In a small way I couldn't be happier. It was now time for me to slow down and think.

CHAPTER 27: THE EPILOGUE

The next few months in Mesa were busy and surprising. The story of Kowalski and his brief moment in baseball revived my career. I was given a regular column in the paper and there has been talk of going to syndication, Perkins took over my position and has been doing a bang up job ever since.

The story on the cover up in baseball sent shock waves through the sport. The players were absolved of any wrong doing, since they all paid a price in losing time and money, besides the effects on their career.

My old paper in Chicago offered me my old job back when the story of how I got used came out. I told them to stuff it. If they didn't believe me than and were willing to let me go, I figured I didn't want them either.

Jim Hudson, my old Chicago editor finally got sacked. Part of the blame, it was said, was for not believing me. Other reporters complained of the same thing and he was let go. That explained the job offer but I never wanted to go back.

The owner who white washed the original investigation was

booted out of his ownership and banned from ever owning a team in the sport again.

The Commissioner barely escaped with his job. Also, he hasn't been heard much from these days. He did get the owners to ban any body like Jason from playing again. I guess one good thing in baseball was enough. They can go on fooling the fans once more.

Jason became quite a celebrity since his hit was heard around the world. He has been appearing on talk shows and making endorsements for everything from cereal to baseball bats. The Cubs recognized a good thing when they saw one and hired Kowalski as part of their front office staff in their communication department. He'll never have to see the inside of a warehouse again.

During spring training this year, Jason came down and invited me to his wedding with Gail. They did a lot talking and figured since they found each other again; they planned not to lose each other again. I hope my friend makes it. I wish them well.

Tim took on the job of agent for Jason and took on a few clients more. But his real love is the law and he isn't planning any major changes.

Jerry Morris was invited to spring training this spring and it looks like he'll stay with the parent club. His long journey in the hinterlands of the minor leagues is over.

The only person I had not heard from was from my 'ex' wife Brenda. I did not hear from the courts, her lawyer, or, from mine, for months. When I tried to call Brenda up, she was never home. I figured she was just busy and didn't have time to give me a call back. Things, I assumed, were back to normal.

One morning as I got into work I got a surprise of my life. Sitting by my desk was Brenda. "You're right, this city is hot. Not sticky, though."

"When did you arrive in town and why are you here?" I was still shocked.

Brenda sighed. "I arrived last night on the red eye. Hope you don't mind."

She asked me if I could get away for a while and talk. I said sure, figuring it was about the divorce and a settlement.

So I took her out for breakfast at a nearby coffee shop down the street from the paper. It was a quiet place at this time of the morning. It was after rush hour and all the reporters that hang out there with some of their sources would not be in for a few hours yet.

After getting out order in and getting out coffee, she announced. "I left my job at the hospital."

She explained to me that the hospital wanted to make a deal with her after the death of that patient.

For months the hospital let her continue to work claiming that they were still investigating the matter. Then one day the administrator called her to his office.

He offered her a deal. She could remain on the staff of the hospital after a one-month suspension. When she came back, she would not come back to the same job, but would be a staff nurse in one of the other units with a cut in pay. He said he was doing this because of her years at the hospital, but, if it anyone else he would have let them go.

She then told the administrator to forget it. "I had done a good job for all those years. I gave up a lot, even my marriage. If that's what you think of me, then you can do without me."

Again, she sighed. "I always loved that job, the excitement, the responsibility, the prestige was what that job was all about. I also loved seeing patients get well. Sometimes that made my day more than any honor or check could ever provide."

"I thought about what you said in Chicago. You said that living here had brought you peace and happiness. You started your life over here and learned to love it. No place is perfect, we both know. But, I thought, if you can walk away from everything and find happiness again, maybe I an do the same thing."

" So, maybe you can show me what is so special here. Do you mind having me as a guest for a while?"

"I'd be glad to have you as a guest, maybe more later on?"

So she moved back in with me and we started to get our marriage back in order. She found a job working as a nurse in the public school system. It wasn't the same or as big as the job in Chicago, but life became simpler for each of us and the rewards were greater than any thing found in any big city.

That's about all I can say for now. All the by-lines have been written and all the deadlines met. Maybe we'll find each other again when the important story has to be written, except....

As spring arrives, baseball season is starting again. The grass is getting greener and the vines at Wrigley are beginning to perk up. When you go to a game this summer, tell them about this story. Just to add a little fantasy, tell them you were there.

.

www.ingramcontent.com/pod-product-compliance
Lightning Source LLC
Chambersburg PA
CBHW052136170626
46812CB00004B/1441